RAPTOR RISING

Anjali Joshi grew up in Mumbai. Her penchant for unexpected twists in her tales can be squarely blamed on the childhood summers spent in her ancestral home. A place full of secret corridors, cupboards and books.

A five-year stint as an air hostess, spent mostly staring down at passing continents and oceans from thirty thousand feet, taught her that the earth knows no borders. And so the mind humbly opened to accept all that the ether chose to download into it. There is a rightful place for both the profound and the profane.

Anjali has over two decades of experience in filmmaking—as a designer, visualizer, editor, writer, producer and director. She is an international expert in 3D holography, clocking over four thousand shows. She currently lives with her two daughters in Hyderabad, India.

Connect with her at:
Instagram: Anjali._._.joshi
Twitter: @_anjalijoshi
Facebook: https://www.facebook.com/anjali.joshi.54738>

Raptor Rising
The Duel Begins

Anjali Joshi

RUPA

Published by
Rupa Publications India Pvt. Ltd 2021
7/16, Ansari Road, Daryaganj
New Delhi 110002

Sales centres:
Allahabad Bengaluru Chennai
Hyderabad Jaipur Kathmandu
Kolkata Mumbai

Copyright © Anjali Joshi 2021

All rights reserved.

No part of this publication may be reproduced, transmitted,
or stored in a retrieval system, in any form or by any means,
electronic, mechanical, photocopying, recording or otherwise,
without the prior permission of the publisher.

This is a work of fiction. Names, characters, places and incidents are either the
product of the author's imagination or are used fictitiously and any resemblance to
any actual person, living or dead, events or locales is entirely coincidental.

ISBN: 978-93-89967-83-8

First impression 2021

10 9 8 7 6 5 4 3 2 1

The moral right of the author has been asserted.

Printed at Thomson Press India Ltd, Faridabad

This book is sold subject to the condition that it shall not,
by way of trade or otherwise, be lent, resold, hired out, or otherwise
circulated, without the publisher's prior consent, in any form of
binding or cover other than that in which it is published.

Salute...
To Aai (Meena), Baba (Surendra) and Shantanu, for their unquestioning love and acceptance.
To my young daughters, Anusha and Priyamvada, for being the amazingly evolved and big-hearted beings they are.

To that energy within...
whose immense beauty and intensity overwhelms me...
halts my steps and permits me to fall into the deepest silence.

Contents

1. Plop…a Drop — 1
2. Bitten — 10
3. Alpha — 12
4. Allure — 15
5. Search — 27
6. Zameer Ka Baap — 31
7. Standup — 35
8. IG — 42
9. Twisted — 46
10. Alibi — 51
11. Talk to Me — 57
12. Pancakes — 61
13. Butt on Fire — 64
14. Pixel — 66
15. Wall of Possibilities — 69
16. Watching You — 73
17. Moustache — 77
18. Is It? — 79
19. New Normal — 82
20. Habit… Repeat — 86
21. Timeline — 90
22. Insider — 91
23. Non Sync — 96
24. I — 103
25. Amazon — 110
26. Cringe — 113
27. Lurker — 115
28. Eeky — 123

29	Bonded	127
30	Father	130
31	Testing Times	133
32	Past Continuous	138
33	Abbot	141
34	The Passing	145
35	Whirr	147
36	Mindfuck	154
37	@Kong	157
38	The Beginning	160
39	Silence	163
40	Kīlauea	166
41	Hold the Gaze	170
42	Rossane	174
43	Rising Demons	177
44	Overmatched	179
45	To See You	181
46	Student	184
47	Garou	188
48	Kill Street	191
49	Sunshine	195
50	Love	199
51	Raptor Rising	205
52	Freedom	211

| *Epilogue* | 214 |
| *Acknowledgements* | 216 |

1

Plop...a Drop

10.5700 degree North; 72.6300 degree East or thereabouts. The Lakshadweep archipelago. A Cessna Citation X comes in low over the Laccadive Sea. Skimming over the northern mangrove encrusted tip of Craig Island.

In the mangroves is a particularly bored Barau's Petrel, its long arched wings folded over its pristine white belly. Heavy headed from the high sun. Scoffing at the advances of an inept male, uncaring of her duties towards the endangered species. The pair are occasionally startled by the loud metallic squawks originating a few hundred metres inland.

A few hundred metres inland...is a forgotten shipping yard, with its precariously positioned, abandoned shipping containers. Painted in psychedelic colours and arranged in a crazy tangle, to look like the coolest interpretation of Dante's hell. The expression of half a dozen art students on a marijuana-laden summer break.

A hooded runner, in a grey CK hoodie, parkour run-jumps over the twisted cables, broken industrial crane arms and onto the roof of a forty-feet shipping container. Another man, tattooed and overmuscled, appears from behind a tangle of cables and confronts him. His rhythm unbroken, the runner proceeds to beat the shit out of the muscled man. The studs on his biker's gloves double up as battering knuckles. Then he unceremoniously flings the muscled man over the left side.

As if on cue, another man appears. He too is a protein-shakes and steroid-fed mass of bulging muscles and veins. He too is battered and sent flying, this time over the right edge of the container.

The hooded runner is not done, he seemingly defies gravity and jump-walks up several more containers. He is barely inches away from getting on to the roof of the last one…when a curved knife swings out over the edge.

The razor-sharp tip of the knife grazes the skin of the runner's forehead, leaving a minuscule jagged cut in the epidermis. A few blood vessels break, spurting tiny droplets of blood. The runner doesn't flinch. Swinging his right foot over the edge, in a single fluid movement, he lands on the roof. The knife-holding attacker and he face-off, with grunts and over-agressive postures.

As their fight begins, a string of drone-mounted movie cameras aligns itself around the men. The 'fight' is being filmed. The runner and his attackers are actors in an action scene. On the ground below, the filming and action crew huddle over the controls. The drone cameras live-feed a series of monitors. The operators move rapidly to make sure each drone stays out of the viewing field of the other drones.

Fight master Roger watches the multiple televisions and barks orders on a megaphone, 'One… Two…elbow…bamm… Three…kick…whoosh…perfect…knife… Left, swing, you motherfucker… Yes, yes…'

Roger is a swarthy, self-serving and perpetually insecure fifty-year-old 'director of action', in other words, a fight master. Raghunath Malhar Pendse, his name was not 'posh' enough, so he started calling himself Roger. Lately, he had met too many pet German Shepherds who shared his name and it made him squirm.

On the roof, completely out of Roger's direct line of sight, the two men follow his commands. The 'motherfucker' does as he is told. The hooded runner lands the kicks on cue. Roger screams,

'Die bastard, die... Aargh.'

The final goon takes up the super exaggerated scream of pain or anger or whatever, pretends to buckle under the hooded runner's kick, goes flying over the edge of the container and lands in a heap on the padded safety boxes forty feet below.

The fight may have been 'mock' but the hooded runner's ability and 'alpha male' postures are for real. The drone cameras following ceaselessly, the runner now pulls off a final parkour stunt and jumps off an incredible height. He makes a perfect three-point landing on the hard ground. The cameras hover behind him. The hooded runner holds the stance. Head bent low to conceal his face. A drop of sweat starts its downward journey from the hairline, it mingles with a drop of blood from the cracked skin on the temple, trickles further down. Plop, it drops on the ground and stays there. Like a full stop.

Roger yells, 'Cut!' The shot is over, the drones turn away and are claimed by their operators. The hooded runner, still on the ground, catches his breath and lifts his head.

It's not a man at all. It's a young woman, strong features, hard eyes with reddened blood vessels. Her nostrils flared with the exertion. She allows herself a smile. Rumana Dhawan knows she has given a great shot.

Fifty feet away is a metallic black augmented vanity van. It looks like an intimidating beast, it is designed to look that way. Everything about it says 'power', 'masculine' and 'aggression'. Inside the van is a man, looking out of the large glass one-way window. He has been closely observing the shoot outside.

Rumana stands up, instinctively looks towards the van. Then she walks away checking out the few bruises she has collected on her parkour run. The crowd gathered 'to watch the shoot', claps for her. They haven't realized that the stunt was performed by a woman. Some unit members, the fake goons and assistants thump her on the back with genuine appreciation. The goon, whose knife barely missed her, approaches a bit sheepishly. She laughs it off with the natural camaraderie of professionals who do risky things every day. The crew gets to work on the next shot.

The man inside the vanity van has digested it all. He puts on a grey CK hoodie, a replica of the one Rumana is wearing.

Rumana steps behind a makeshift tent and strips. Not just her clothes but also the bulky bodysuit underneath. The sculpted suit, that made her appear large, manly and muscular. She reveals a stunningly sexy and well-toned muscular body, startlingly different from her earlier avatar. Two junior stuntmen goofing around with some safety harnesses, respectfully slink out of the place, giving her the privacy she doesn't seem to need.

The man in the vanity van has waited just long enough for the attention around Rumana to wane. With a flourish, he opens the van door and steps out.

This is Zameer Khan, the Bollywood superstar, an extremely handsome man with a striking alpha male attitude. The crowd has been waiting for this moment. A spontaneous cheer rises from all directions. He waves back in acknowledgement. Instantly, a retinue of staff, hopeful-future-producers, and his secretary, Honey, rush to him.

Honey keeps muttering something to him. The makeup man fusses over him, spraying fake sweat and fake blood drops. The costume assistant gives him a replica of the biker gloves Rumana had been wearing. The film's director, Preet Singh, shoos everyone away.

Preet is a forty-three-year-old closeted bisexual with a perfectly sculpted pencil moustache and transplanted hair. As usual, his body is squeezed into a pair of Diesel jeans that are one size too small for him. He shouts at the makeup man. 'You idiot! Stop killing his glamour, how much sweat do you want to put on him?'

With a flourish, Zameer Khan starts getting down into an identical three-point landing pose struck by his dupe Rumana. He is already performing before the camera starts rolling. He is performing for the crowds beyond the barricades. The audience cheers him as though he were an Olympic hundred-metre race world champion dropping into a start position.

And then, as he is about to place his gloved hand on the ground, his eyes catch sight of Rumana's minuscule pink blood-sweat drop, just millimetres away from where his fingers need to be placed.

His smug performance cracks, he recoils as though stung. He glares at the tiny pink drop as though it is the black plague. His staff crowds around and fall over themselves to peer at it. Zameer Khan hisses under his breath, 'Which fucking pig fucked up here? It is so fucking unhygienic. How the fuck am I supposed to work?'

Zameer's sentence construction skills were mostly limited to using the word 'fuck' as a substitute for almost all other words. He is a whisker away from heading back to the van…but hasn't because of the large crowd behind the barricade.

The film's producer, Sharman, supremely sensitive to Zameer's fluctuating moods, swings into action. He barges into the tent where Rumana is changing. He starts ticking her off, making sure he is loud enough for Zameer Khan to hear.

'What were you thinking? Don't you know how to behave around a star? Who brought you in? Where is Zameer's regular dupe?'

Rumana is taken aback, doesn't quite know why she is being shouted at. The action master, Roger, steps in, 'She is really talented, didn't you see, she gave the shot in one take…anyone else would have wasted half your day to get it right. Go, Rumana, apologize to Zameer Khan…it won't happen again…'

Rumana is doing her best to cover her humiliation. She comes out of the tent and walks up to Zameer Khan.

'Sorry, I didn't realize…'

She goes down on her knees and dabs the drop with a tissue. Zameer Khan suddenly realizes that this girl was his dupe. He also becomes conscious of the crowd trying to figure out the drama. He wonders if this is going to make him look bad. First, a woman dupe, then kneeling at his feet in this manner. One Instagram, or a Snapchat post by some trigger-happy arsehole… He quickly brings her to a standing position.

'Arre, don't worry. That fucker Sharman is making too much of it…'

She walks away, shoulders slumped, a far cry from the alpha male posture she had adopted to make Zameer Khan look good in the action sequence. Zameer Khan gets down into position once again. Adjusts his face and breathes as though he has just finished the parkour run himself.

The camera rolls. Action. Zameer Khan dramatically lifts his head, the hood slips back to reveal his face. His eyes are burning with energy. The hazel brown eyes with flecks of gold that make a million women swoon. The result of custom-made contact lenses. He flares his nostril just that little bit as he pants a couple of times from the imagined exertion of the parkour run he never executed.

'Cut. Great shot! Zameer, only you can give a shot like that bro!' Director Preet gushes, the fans behind the barricades cheer. Zameer ignores them and heads to his vanity van.

Assistant director Mahesh whispers to Preet, 'His face is looking too fresh, sir, needs more sweat'.

Preet knows he is right. 'Make a note, put sweat drops in CG'.

Producer Sharman Singh, perpetually eavesdropping on everybody who matters, overhears the exchange and snorts in displeasure. Mutters under his breath, 'Fucking chut, wasting my CG budget on sweat drops…'

Inside the action team's tent, Roger gestures to Rumana that she is done for the day. Rumana asks, 'What time do I come tomorrow?' Roger gives her a sharp look of dismissal. Rumana persists, 'but you promised…' He shrugs, 'I gave you a break when you aren't even a stuntwoman…' Rumana cuts him, a hard edge of anger building up inside her, 'That you did because I am bloody good, better than any of your guys can ever be.'

He displays a sudden burst of aggression wanting to quell the imposing Rumana, 'What the fuck were you expecting? You paid me to get you close to Zameer, I did! You blew it, woman. You want to get into his pants…find another way, now get lost.'

Roger hears his name being called by the director on the megaphone and uses it as an excuse to leave. Mahesh has seen the exchange between them. He strolls up to Rumana and hands her a cup of tea. Overtly, it's just a friendly gesture. But his beady eyes say something else.

Rumana acknowledges his move with an almost imperceptible nod. Her eyes are fixed on the vanity van with Zameer Khan in it. She leaves. As she passes through the crowd, a couple of groupie girls cheer and hug her. She is distant and pulls herself away.

Zameer Khan steps out for his next shot. The crowd starts calling out to him and cheering wildly again.

Sharman shouts, 'Hey, keep them quiet!'

Mahesh heads for the two local cops, Samuel and Roddy, who are supposed to be handling the crowds but are chatting up the junior action guys. 'Hey, keep them quiet!'

The cops bristle, make their way to the barricades and yell at the crowds, 'Hey, keep quiet!'

The cops sulk. 'We give them permission to shoot in our town and they order us around,' mutters Samuel.

The unit breaks for lunch. The warmth of the overhead sun and the humidity has sapped everybody. The cops start trailing behind the senior unit members into the restaurant, only to be accosted by Mahesh, 'Chill, uncle. Giving us the permissions warmed your pocket too. And look what it did for your island. All hotels sold out, tons of publicity, what are you complaining about?'

Mahesh leads them into a shanty set up on the beach. They find themselves amongst the junior crew, lightmen, stuntmen and background artists. Around them, large rotis are being ripped and dipped in oily fish gravies. It's only grime, no glamour. They squirm. They had hoped to be within the enchanted circle of the senior shooting unit that is chilling in the plush restaurant, downing colourful mocktails and piling up food in their plates from the seemingly endless buffet.

On the other side of the road, perched at a vantage point in an exclusive terrace lounge, Rumana is watching the unit. The sweaty dupe look is gone. She is dressed in a casually expensive manner and looks completely at home. The staff maintains a respectful distance. Her vodka martini is untouched. The minuscule cut on her forehead has been covered with makeup. It is her nature to be on the prowl and she knows it. The chase is as essential as the kill.

Her eyes smoulder as she looks at Zameer Khan's vanity van.

A black Porsche pulls up. Shilpa, the stunningly beautiful heroine of the film steps out. Delicate, extremely feminine and graceful. As if on cue, the door of the vanity van opens and she steps in. The whole operation happens so quickly that it probably goes unnoticed from the ground. But from her vantage point, Rumana takes it all in.

Then she heads for the spa. She is escorted straight into a room. The walls are clad with muted-coloured silk. A single skylight with smoked glass permits soft light to filter in. The room is a cocoon of silence.

She settles on the silk-layered bed. Jasmine, the therapist enters noiselessly with a tray of freshly made scrubs and packs. Rumana can detect the faint scent of kiwi, avocado, crushed rose petals… Jasmine ignites the mild camphor stick and the fragrance takes over.

The therapist smothers her face with a series of lotions, Rumana relaxes. The overheated facial skin starts cooling off, as the therapist's fingers move with precision over every contour and crevice of her face. The muscles slacken. Eyes closed, Rumana allows herself to sink into the silence. At some point, she dozes off.

The therapist continues wiping and slathering Rumana's skin with a range of lotions and pastes.

2

Bitten

Late evening. 'The Palms', with its unimaginative name, is the nightclub in the island's biggest resort. The name was its legacy from the long-gone guest house that had once been the favourite haunt of hippies in the '70s.

Music spills out through the large doors onto the lawn. Rumana and a few girls are trying to pole dance around a lamp post. They are high, as is the rest of the crowd. No one seems to even notice their shenanigans.

Mahesh notices her from across the bar.

Mahesh, at thirty, had realized that he would never make his masterpiece as a director. He was never the angst type. He would rather make the most of whatever the heat of the moment brings his way. He is here, hoping to make something out of his silent exchange with Rumana earlier in the day.

He walks up to her, wraps himself around her as though it's the perfectly natural thing to do. Through the haze, she registers him and lets him grind against her.

Rumana asks, 'How is this going to help me?'

Mahesh is too caught up in the grinding, he can't think up a smart reply.

'Will this get me a part in the film? Right next to Zameer Khan?'

Mahesh is ready to agree to anything at this point. He grunts and nods.

'To touch him, to feel him…to smell him…to eat him,' she demands.

Suddenly she is coming on with a kinky ferocity. Her nails claw into his thighs. Her lips start a kiss that instantly transforms into a vice-like grip on his lower lip, with her teeth sinking into the soft flesh.

He looks straight into her dead dark eyes that show no sign of the violence her body is inflicting on him. Mahesh, whose only intention was to have a bit of fun, is taken aback. This woman is crazy. He is squirming and twitching, trying to pull away. She is still biting his lip, not letting go. Mahesh panics, she seems intent on ripping his lip off if he tries to back off.

Then she suddenly lets go, he stumbles and instantly moves to a safe distance. There are sharp bright crimson teeth marks on his lower lip. Surprisingly, her teeth didn't break through the skin and make him bleed. Rumana turns away, moving back to her friends. She is swaying gently to the new number that's begun, no sign of the violence from a moment ago. Mahesh makes his way to the bar, throwing back an occasional look. He is glad to be getting away.

3

Alpha

Early next morning, a young woman in a striking neon blue summer dress walks down the pier to a boat. There isn't a trace of the sleepless night on her face. She is wearing a sun hat in anticipation of the warm day ahead and is carrying a largish back-to-basics bag slung over her shoulder.

Two beach boys, cleaning up their shack, wave to her. One calls out with unexpected familiarity, 'Madam, Rumana madam… morning is a good time to catch them…fish.'

The other one adds, 'The dolphins, let me show you, they will be dancing.'

She laughs at their crude invitations and blows them a kiss, her ease with their assumed familiarity is surprising. The fact that she doesn't care, projects a sense of power. She has obviously fucked both of them, enjoyed it and doesn't care who knows it. She gets into a boat with a small yet distinctive maple leaves insignia on it.

The insignia was designed especially for Rumana's father, Rakesh Dhawan's global chain of resorts. There are two other boats with similar insignia, tied to the jetty and bobbing in the waves nearby. Folks who didn't like Dhawan, which was a substantial crowd for sure…and folks who tolerated him, always wondered how his progeny could be so dramatically unlike him. On his good days, he looked like an overdone rice dumpling. Dhawan adored his little girl, though lately it had been tinged with an undefinable unease.

In a matter of minutes, Rumana starts the ignition and heads out to sea. The sun is not up yet and she disappears into the sea haze quickly. The beach boys watch her go. No luck this morning.

Out in the ocean, Red Reef isle, a favourite nesting spot of the herring gulls. A private island with its solitary villa, it was once the love pad of an aviation magnet now gone broke. Rented out to the very few who can afford it.

Zameer is in a large bed with Shilpa. He wakes up, gets on top of her and starts ripping off her flimsy negligee roughly. She wakes up with a start, almost winces, then cleverly covering it up with a sigh, pretends to enjoy it. A consummate actress, her beauty undermines her talent. For the super conceited Zameer, a few strategic moans and gasps are all that's needed of her.

In the boat, Rumana is within sight of the island. She is scanning it with a powerful pair of binoculars. A pale pre-dawn light is filtering into the open east-facing bedroom. She spots the couple making out. She lingers on the stunningly beautiful Shilpa. Zameer's undisguised brute force is palpable even at this distance. She is mesmerized by it. She watches closely, studying it, studying him. It was an incredible opportunity she could never have hoped for.

The boat is now as close as she can take it. No time to watch any more, it's time to get ready. The unpleasant exchange with Zameer on the film set plays out in her mind. It makes her pensive. Then coming to a decision, she shuts the engine and brings the boat to a halt. She drops the anchor then heads into the cabin, humming to herself.

She pulls out a bright crimson bikini and a wrap from the bag. She ties her hair back and looks quizzically at her face in the mirror.

Back in the villa, Shilpa is feigning satiated exhaustion and sleep. Well aware of the fragility of her body, she has no intentions of letting Zameer or any of these mandatory lovers scar her in any manner.

Zameer is still raring to go. He looks down at her in disdain if that's all he is going to get out of her he might as well burn the rest with a jog on the beach. As he leaves, he turns to look at her once again.

He had agreed to the film only if she would spend six months faking a love affair with him. Their picture-perfect looks were already creating a buzz he liked. Her childlike virginal face on the much-used body fills him with sudden contempt. The contempt that comes from knowing that she was no different than him. He had bartered his body no less in his scramble to the top of the heap. Till he became the alpha male, the apex predator. It felt good on the top. He planned to stay there for a long time.

4

Allure

On the boat, Rumana discards her blue outfit. From her bag, she pulls out a couple of bottles, tubes and other makeup paraphernalia. She places them neatly on a desk. She picks up a glass bottle with a spray nozzle. She sprays a few drops of the liquid on her inner wrist. The droplets dry instantly and form a smooth luminescent golden tanned film, it covers up every tiny blemish and the naturally varying tone of her skin. It is almost like spraying on a second skin. A skin that is several shades more tanned.

Satisfied with the result, she sprays her entire body. The liquid settles and dries onto her pores. She tests the colour again and again with her fingers, to ensure that it does not come off.

The loops of the red swimsuit get hooked, the knot of her wrap is tied. Fingers flip open a box to reveal some exotic pieces of jewellery. She pulls out an ornament. A large dark stone set in a cluster of jewels. She clips it on, the stone now rests between her breasts, kept in place by a harness winding around her neck and ribs. It's a tantalizing mix between a bondage harness and art jewellery.

Her incessant humming stops momentarily as she goes to work on her face. She chooses a bright peach-coloured lipstick that looks startling against her bronzed skin.

Back on the deck, she is at the wheel. One hand goes to the back of her head and removes the clasp that was holding the hair away from her face. The wind catches the long tresses, tosses the curls around. Her hair is still the deep burgundy with highlights of gold, but her face is completely transformed.

The woman who started as Rumana, now not only has a new skin but also a completely new face.

The features are soft and feminine, the strong jaw and high cut cheekbones are gone. Her eyes are full of mischief and there is a smile playing on her gloss moistened peach lips. There is a lightness in her being that's hard to imagine of the brooding Rumana.

Ahead of her, just over eight hundred metres away, is the northern tip of the island, out of the villa's line of sight. She heads towards a sheltered cove.

Inside the villa, a relieved Shilpa has fallen asleep for real.

Zameer runs down the steps of an artificial rock garden and on to the patio leading to the sand. He is dressed for a jog. He starts a series of warm-up exercises.

He bears an uncanny resemblance to his great grandfather, or so he had been told. Over a century ago, fifteen-year-old Atiq Khan made his way through the Irshad Pass, and on to Karachi. Traversing the badlands, he had suffered and inflicted violence in equal measure. He never spoke about it, a boy just had to do what he needed to do.

On the eve of the India–Pakistan Partition, the now prosperous Atiq took a seemingly suicidal decision to sail to the enemy's land. With his fleet of fifteen dhows, he reached the port of Mumbai. A move that paid off beyond his expectations.

Zameer was born without any imprint of the family's history. He didn't really give a fuck about the long-dead man. He was just happy to have inherited the northern frontier good looks that Bollywood salivated over.

Lately, he had found himself fascinated by the charcoal sketches

Atiq Khan had left behind, of his final memories of the Irshad Pass. Zameer felt inside him an uncharacteristic urge to stand in the very same spot as young Atiq. It disturbed Zameer, even frightened him, this nostalgic mush reaching him across generations. Was he getting old?

Even now, the thought creates a slight disturbance that interrupts his warm-up regimen. He stops to take a sip of water. A flash of colour momentarily appears in a break in the palms encircling the patio. It distracts him. He catches sight of a figure at the water's edge, it seems to be a sexy-looking woman in a crimson bathing suit.

The woman is playing in the waves and striking sensual poses. He can't see her face but the body language conveys that she knows he is watching and this is for him.

Zameer makes a call on his mobile to Sharman, 'Fucker, I thought this island was uninhabited...' Sharman answers groggily, 'It is.' Zameer laughs. Sharman also laughs a hollow fake laugh, not knowing why Zameer laughed but echoing it nonetheless.

Zameer drops the phone on the garden table and sets off after the woman. For him, this is routine. One more stunning woman chasing him, wanting to get laid by him. This one is exceptionally sexy. And he is game.

The woman laughs warmly when she sees him make a beeline for her. It's an instant silent pact between strangers.

She teases him, running down the sand at the edge of the water. He chases her. She lets him grab her wrap as she runs. He rubs it to his face, sniffing, kissing, laughing then drops it into the water. He is enjoying the chase. It's dreamy, romantic, picture-perfect, near-naked Adam and Eve in the Garden of Eden.

The same surrealism continues when her wrap seems to dissolve in the seawater and within moments, disappears completely.

Zameer is amused by the unexpected trick as he sees it disappear. She lets him catch up. They make out for a bit at the edge of the waves. Displacing the sand and scaring a few baby brachyuran crabs.

She laughs, her eyes light up. Then she slips out of his grasp and runs again. Now she is just a little bit faster than he anticipated. The mock chase was fun, but this needs more effort. An irritation is already building up inside Zameer. They reach a small lagoon. She dives and swims across the lagoon to a sand bar with a coconut grove. He follows, now determined. She runs over a patch of sand, he takes a short cut over some rocks.

She slows down, he leaps forward and grabs her finally. He is full of violence and heat, rips off her remaining garment. The bathing suit is in shreds. He is somehow transformed. Zameer likes to play but he doesn't like being played, and this woman had stretched him more than he liked. Well, now she is going to get a taste of the real Zameer Khan.

Reflecting the change in him…something inside her is also turning. He possesses her with a merciless edge that begins to gnaw. Extreme passion bestows beauty on some faces, others it distorts into ugliness. From the perfect 'hero', he is transforming into a nasty bully.

The seductive pout goes sour on her face, freezes, for a fleeting moment. She blinks. Rapid visions run in her mind: different time, different faces, yet the same unmistakable look of ugliness and depravity.

His brain is jammed by the avalanche of senses, he is unstoppable, he has her over-powered and he is going to make the most of it.

She laughs unexpectedly and arches her body, pressing it closer to him, an act of deliberate teasing defiance. He will prove a worthy partner in this duel.

Zameer is surprised. So the bitch likes it, after the bland picture-perfect Shilpa, this woman is just what he needs. It must be the scoundrel Sharman's doing. He must have sent her. Well, the man knows how to treat his star right!

Zameer's weight behind each thrust is pushing her into the sand. Her hand gropes, trying to grab for support as he hammers into her.

Her fingers are prodding through the sand. She finds something, a bracelet. It's a singular delicate-looking *shakudo* bracelet with a beautiful blue-grey sheen. She arches her torso, lifting it off the ground, stretches her arms way behind her back, out of his line of sight and snaps it on. The heads of two mythical beasts with elongated bodies now make a circle around her wrist. One beast-head is turned upward, jaws wide open, inch-long needle-thin diamond fangs protrude menacingly.

The ferocity and frequency of Zameer's thrusts are increasing rapidly, displacing her inch by inch. She adjusts her body under him, aligning her spine to his, this allows her to lock her ankles behind him and pull him even closer. She lifts her hips upwards, keeping to his rhythm. Zameer is flattered that she seems to enjoy the violence.

The involuntary gloating makes him falter for a fraction of a second. It's her opening.

With a manic force, her palms land on the small of his back and pull him in even tighter. His back arches at her sudden thrust. Her left leg around him tightens further. The right leg unwinds and she places it firmly in the sand. And then with an animal grunt, she tightens her core muscles, keeping his centre of gravity exactly above her hips, she thrusts upwards, lifts him straight off the ground.

His body rises, legs loosen their grip on her thighs. In a rapid fluid movement, she moves in an arch around him, and…thud! lands him flat on his back, with her on top, pinning him down.

Zameer's eyes fly open in shock as he lands on the sand. Despite himself, he has a stunned, moronic grin on his face. This complete powerlessness is a new experience for him.

The rhythm of her grind never slips, her palms and fingers are moving relentlessly on his upper body. His irregular guttural moaning and gasping sounds like a beast, far from human. The caressing changes and she lands swift sharp blows on his neck and torso with the side of her palms. Each time she makes contact, Zameer lets out a gasp. The avalanche of pain and pleasure seems to be short-circuiting Zameer's brain. His body is becoming malleable, all muscles loosening.

Thhuck! The close-fisted blow lands straight on his heart. Zameer's entire body jumps up. He gags, his breath freezes and his eyes mist over.

This crazy woman has taken him into a zone he cannot fathom. Control, the all-important control, it just slipped out of his hands.

And then…as a finale to this beastly symphony of sex, she draws her hands to her sides, elbows bent. She unleashes them with blinding speed, centre and index fingers extended, straight at Zameer's neck.

As they make first contact, his neck seems to buckle and curve inwards, next instant, unexpectedly, the fingers break through the skin and muscles barrier. They plunge straight in, like the talons of a raptor.

In a fraction she yanks out the jugular vein on the right and the carotid artery on the left…Snap, crimson blood spurts nearly a foot into the air.

In the extended heightened time awareness, Zameer realizes

he is already dead, his eyes widen, as her torso against the now burning sky seems to morph into a dark expanding cloud… engulfing him…and then his eyes glaze over.

Blood and bits of tissue still trailing from her nails, she arches her back and screams a soundless scream into the azure blue clear morning skies. The blood is gushing out, flowing down the slope to the waves barely a few feet away.

The frenzy of the kill is over, but her body is still vibrating with its extreme energy. Sweat pours down her skin from the exertion, breath comes out in soft rasps. With slightly wobbly knees she gets to her feet.

She heads into the waves leaving his body on the sand. She dives in. The water cleans the blood from her skin. Swirls of crimson rapidly form and dissipate in the water. Gathering fistfuls of sand from the seafloor, she rubs herself all over, removing every trace of him.

When she rises out of the waves she is completely cleansed, her skin glistens with a pristine quality in the sunlight. She is strangely calm.

She sits cross-legged on the wet sand, closes her eyes and goes into an instant deep meditation. Her complete serenity, in close proximity of the blood-spewing kill, is chilling.

The tide is coming in rapidly, the waves rushing up the sand, they seem almost eager to clean up for her. The blood from the sand is disappearing with each rising wave.

The waves are also wiping out the final traces of Zameer and her footsteps on the wet sand, on the beach as she led him to the spot.

She gets up. Her equilibrium is back. A flock of herring gulls has started circling overhead, ready to swoop down on the carcass. High above them, two Amur falcons have just arrived. News of the fresh-kill travels fast on nature's grapevine.

She ties a rope to Zameer's leg. Drags it into the water. The gulls screech in disappointment. She smiles.

She ties the other end of the rope to a rubber raft concealed nearby. The body half sinks, half floats. Tiny orange clownfish, with big black eyes, excitedly rush to the feast. She returns to the site of the killing.

She pulls out the bag concealed behind a rock, loosely puts on another wrap. Next, she pulls out an iPad. She rapidly scrolls through the open interphase, it is a customized video editing software. She is scanning the footage of the killing, captured by a series of cameras concealed in the surrounding area.

She not only killed him, but also filmed the whole act from several angles.

Thirty minutes ago.

She lands on the isolated stretch of sand on a rubber raft and conceals it under some overhanging rocks. She moves rapidly and precisely. She sets up four concealed cameras, mounted on the palm tree trunks and amidst thickset undergrowth. She adjusts their angles and focus: two are set to a wide frame taking in the whole area. Two zoomed in at the exact spot she needs to bring Zameer to, for precise framing.

Next, she buries the *shakudo* bracelet where she can find it later. Finally, she erases her footprints on the sand. Satisfied with her arrangements she sets out to the southern face of the island, to the villa and Zameer.

With uncanny discipline and precision, she had lured him to the exact spot she needed him to be. Perfect centre framing, an actor's delight. And then she had extracted out of him the performance of a lifetime.

She is editing on the fly, creating a clip that shows the entire act cleverly in its raw sexuality and violence. She ensures that her face is never visible, her identity is never revealed in any manner. The reason for the detailed cover-up of her skin tone and the change in her face is now evident. She is not going to take any chances, she has no intention of being caught.

She opens a small box, nestled in it is a drone-like object. She operates it with the remote. It starts moving over the sand.

Her bracelet goes into another box and is sealed. The large dark stone of the jewellery harness comes off revealing a miniature camera. That was the fifth camera which shot the extreme close-up of Zameer's dying face and spurting jugular. She packs it up.

The rest of the cameras are dismantled. All clear. With clinical precision, she has sanitized the place. The tide has risen rapidly. The waves are already running over the spot where Zameer was killed. In moments, the tide will cover it completely.

Just before she leaves, she puts on a pair of gloves. From a ziploc bag, she pulls out fish innards and scatters them on the sand. A parting gift for the gulls, who shriek, swoop and squabble to get the tasty bits. She laughs softly as she watches them for a few moments. The energy of the kill has dissipated so completely that it may not have happened at all.

She starts the rubber raft to get back to her boat. Zameer's body is suddenly yanked into motion and dragged behind the raft. The reef fish find their meal rushing off, they chase for a bit, then fall back.

The raft soon meets the boat in anchor nearly a kilometre into the ocean.

Under the water, Zameer's body is trailing face down. Suddenly, it stops, floats listlessly. A translucent plastic body bag is lowered and slides over him, encircling his entire body. Swish. The bag contracts, all air and water is sucked out and it shrink-wraps tightly around him. His distorted face with the proud Afghan nose protruding ghoulishly from inside the tightened polybenzimidazole.

Sealed in the super-strong material, used by NASA to make suits for astronauts. All odours and tastes that his decaying body will give out are now contained in this shroud. It will keep the predators away. It will keep discovery away.

An indeterminate shape starts rapidly coming closer, now close enough it is revealed to be a weight. It swishes past Zameer. For a few moments, Zameer's body continues floating, then with a violent jerk, it is pulled away and rushes deep into the dark depths of the sea.

Perhaps, if Zameer had given in to the ancient nostalgia, this spring would have found him at the Irshad Pass, four thousand nine hundred metres above sea level…not heading to the dark marine floor, four thousand metres below.

The rubber raft has been deflated and is drying out on the deck. She steps inside the cabin. A soft mechanical 'whirr' sound can be heard. She is humming as she starts undressing and reaches out for the neon blue dress.

In the villa, Shilpa wakes up, finds Zameer gone. Far in the horizon, the boat disappears. She makes her way through the villa and the gardens, looking for Zameer. She peers out through the broad verandahs, the beach stretches…empty.

On the boat. Rumana is back, in her blue dress and sun hat. The persona that killed Zameer has transformed. The mischief in her eyes is gone, replaced with the old hard glint and the stubborn jaw.

She completes the edit that started on the island. Mulls over it for a few moments, makes a few changes in her film, then selects 'upload' on her handset. Her kill-film starts uploading.

A herring gull calls above, she looks up at it. Then she zips past a fishing trawler, returns to the shore she left earlier that morning.

Shilpa steps out into the rock garden with two mugs of steaming coffee. A herring gull screeches overhead, almost mocking.

Plop. With uncanny precision the gull shits into the coffee mug. Splattering shitty coffee on her manicured fingers, with their glitzy nail art. She drops the mug in disgust.

Shilpa calls Sharman, 'I am not able to find Zameer. I mean, his mobile is here…and…'

Sharman is still in bed, 'Couldn't find? It's a fucking island, where can he go…he called me just a while ago…'

'Yes, but I… I can't see him…'

'For heaven's sake, woman, your only job was to fuck him and keep an eye on him. How could you screw that up?'

He is already marching out of his room in his faux-silk underpants. His ample jelly-belly rolling and spilling over it, his unrestrained balls flapping between his thighs under the extra clingy fabric. His transplanted hair standing like multidirectional porcupine quills on his head. This is not a sight to be inflicted on the unprepared so early in the morning. But he doesn't care, he makes a noisy entry into the hotel corridor.

His two assistants run up to him.

'Get me a boat to go to the island immediately. These stupid women, can't be trusted to do anything right…she can't find Zameer it seems…'

Director Preet pops out from the next room, 'What! Then today's shoot is cancelled?'

'Is there no one else in the film?' asked Sharman. 'Line up

scenes that don't need him. Work cannot stop. Zameer must be chasing some woman...or his secretary will show up haggling for more money.'

As if on cue, the lift door opens, Secretary Honey steps out, digging his teeth with a toothpick. He has overeaten at the breakfast buffet as is his daily habit and plans to get some rest for digestive purposes.

He freezes seeing four pairs of eyes pointed at him like lasers.

'Hey, you, where the hell is Zameer?' Sharman wants to know.

'Huh?'

'You are his secretary...where is he?'

5

Search

The search for Zameer is on.

Half a dozen unit members are climbing rocks and scanning the secluded grooves. The junior-most assistant is made to wade through the now, shoulder-deep waters of the lagoon and cross over to the coconut grove. He plods over the rocks and sands, disturbs some nesting birds in the undergrowth. They squawk loudly in protest. That discourages any further investigation on his part. He gets on the highest rock, surveys, there is nothing to be discovered. The sandbanks look exactly the way they have for millennia.

'Nothing here,' he reports over his walkie-talkie.

Roger is supervising the removal of the two security cameras on the island's jetty. One turns out to be a dummy. The second camera has a chip inside.

Shilpa is perched on the low verandah wall, overlooking the rock garden, wringing her hands and looking distraught for Sharman's sake. Inwardly she is hoping that Zameer is holed up with some oversexed woman who drains him and buys her some breathing space.

Sharman is pacing rapidly in the rock garden. His concealed tummy tucker waist belt, worn in a hurry, has squished his rolling stomach but made him more pigeon-chested than usual. The agitation and high blood pressure have reddened his eyes, his face resembles the inside of an overripe watermelon. He is trying to unlock Zameer's abandoned mobile. Zameer's last conversation with him is playing in his head over and over again.

'...He laughed, the bastard laughed...' Sharman says to Roger.

Roger is staring into the footage of the surveillance camera, 'Shit!'

Sharman hurriedly peers in and realizes that Roger was actually describing what was visible in the footage. Bird shit covered most of the lens. The partially clear area revealed the wooden planks of the jetty flooring directly under the camera perch.

Honey is calling one resort after another, 'Hello! Did Mr Zameer Khan visit...'

Sharman gets a call from the island's small airport. It is Mahesh, 'Morning flight cancelled boss. He didn't fly out. The next flight out is this evening.'

Sharman can only snort, curse and fume, 'Damn him, I am not doing another film with the bastard.'

Roger is amused, 'Zameer is your addiction, Sharman, one that you will never be able to break.'

Back on the main island, the filming has started on the streets. The unit is subdued. Barricades are in place, but there are no crowds to hold back. The beach boys and shack owners are happy, yesterday's gawkers are chilling over beers and hiring boats, driving up the sales.

Samuel and Roddy are hanging around listlessly. Preet is taking some shots with the character artists. Nobody is really interested in them. The cops have nothing to do, nothing to control.

Rumana strolls over to Preet, 'Where is Zameer Khan?'

'Do you think the film has no other actor apart from Zameer Khan? Work is going on, do not disturb,' Preet retorts.

Rumana moves away. Her eye catches a young man sitting under a huge umbrella. The 'second' hero. In Zameer's absence, he is getting a lot of attention. She stops to look him over. One can almost hear the wheels in her mind spinning. Sensing her sharp gaze, the man instinctively turns around. She locks eyes with him, her eyes hold a dark promise.

Cop Samuel gets a call from Sharman.

Samuel plays hard to get, 'What do we know of the ways of the Bollywood demigods? We poor mortals can't even breathe the same air as you guys…'

'What are you saying? We are nothing without you. Who has been misbehaving with you? I will take their arse. But lesser people will do these things. Your presence is critical, Sir. I am sending my Lamborghini, Sir, please come, please come.'

The Lamborghini pulls up on the other side of the barricade. Roddy narrowly misses getting whacked on the nose as its scissor door opens upwards. Samuel pretends to be savvy about 'posh stuff' but gingerly steps in.

The doors ceremoniously close. Samuel and Roddy preen. A few locals and tourist notice it. The car drives a few hundred yards to the wharf, then halts. They take their time getting off, hoping that more locals will notice their elevated status.

This time it's a handful of kids, whose cricket ball barely misses Samuel and the car. The driver lets loose a string of curses at the kids, reserved in honour of the car only. It completely spoils their big moment.

The cops reach the island. Just yesterday they were on the periphery of this exciting world, now they are sitting down with the goddess Shilpa. She looks stunning and suitably tragic. Senior cop Samuel clucks sympathetically and junior cop Roddy takes down her story.

'…and he was gone… I am so distraught… I miss him so much (lets a tear crawl down her cheek artfully). Oh! Zameer, I love you so much, come back, please come back…'

Sharman is not impressed and gives her nasty looks. Zero progress is being made.

Fired by the beautiful Shilpa's performance, brimming with importance, Samuel instructs Roddy, 'Be alert, I want to know even if a fish swims out of our bay!'

To Sharman, 'I will check the airport personally, the only flight to the mainland is this evening and let me assure you, Zameer Khan won't be able to sneak onboard under my keen eyes!'

Then patting Sharman's hand as though he is a man of worldly wisdom, in a conspiratorial tone he continues, 'We will search all the hotels too, Zameer was interested in many girls, my sources tell me. So our law machinery is already at work you see…already at work.'

Sharman's eyes speak very clearly, 'Jerk!'

6

Zameer Ka Baap

Evening. Sharman, Honey, Samuel and Roddy are at the airport. A hall split into two by a low metal barricade serves as the 'arrival' and the 'departure'. Nothing much happens here. Each morning, sixteen passengers land and sixteen depart. The same is repeated each evening. The meagre airport security is in full attendance and is buzzing with excitement; the hush-hush search for Zameer Khan is possibly the highpoint of their entire career.

The outgoing passengers are being put through extreme scrutiny. Sharman to the guards, 'Remember, he could be disguised as anything. The only thing he can't hide about himself is his height.'

All tall men find themselves being frisked and checked over and over again. A man's beard is discreetly tugged, another's paunch is discreetly poked under the guise of a pat-down.

'Prosthetics, they can disguise anything with makeup these days,' cautioned Sharman.

Roddy promptly eyes a tall buxom girl suspiciously, she is next in line for frisking. He makes a beeline for her with the fullest intention of checking out if the bulges on her are real or 'prosthetics'. A lady security guard steps in and leads her behind a partition. Everything is real. The lady passenger is not amused when she catches Roddy trying to align himself with a crack in the partition to get a better view of the frisking inside. She ticks him off and demands to see the security chief.

Last in the line is a grouchy old lady in a wheelchair. In their heightened agitation, they find her suspicious. They try to measure her height in her sitting position. The three strands of hair on her chin bristle with irritation.

The incoming plane lands. The Cessna Citation X with its load of sixteen passengers. They walk across the tarmac and enter the arrival side of the barricade. A trolley trudges across the concrete ferrying the luggage from the aircraft. The captain heads straight for the smoking enclosure. The maintenance engineer steps into the enclosure carrying two bags of the day's best catch straight from the fishing trawler. Hands it over to the captain, then heads for the aircraft. He has twenty minutes to declare it fit for take-off.

Back in the passenger area, the arriving passengers are huddled around the trolley with bags, waiting for the loader to line up the bags on the floor. There is no conveyor belt here.

Over the barricade separating the departure and arrival areas, Samuel catches sight of the grey hoodie-clad back of a tall broad-shouldered man. The figure looks similar to Zameer Khan in the action scene the day before. In a jiffy, Samuel climbs over to the arrival area, makes a beeline for the tall stranger and lands a heavy hand on his shoulder.

'Zameer!'

The man turns, it is not Zameer. Mid-thirties, a youthful smiling face and large expressive dark eyes, startling to look at. A clean-shaven head is revealed under the hood that's slipped off.

Samuel deflates, this cannot possibly be Zameer Khan in disguise.

The man peers back, 'Zameer?'

Samuel mutters weakly, 'Move on, move on, we are looking for Zameer Khan…'

The man catches on, 'Zameer Khan! You thought I was the

Zameer fucking Khan? Of course, I am Zameer Khan...*arre Zameer Khan kya mein toh uske baap ka baap hoon!*'

Samuel walks away, wanting to distance himself from his obvious goof-up. But the stranger is not letting it go. He instantly mimics Zameer Khan's voice perfectly, and dramatically reels out dialogues from his hit films. He even strikes some of Zameer's favourite poses. The raised voice sounding exactly like Zameer Khan makes Sharman jump, he comes rushing. Samuel is trying to calm things down.

Some of the passengers who were on the way out start discussing.

'What's happening?'

'Don't know.'

'I think it's a secret screen test, you know...reality TV and all that stuff...'

'Wow! You are right, that is the producer Sharman...'

Suddenly a young puny passenger from the departure side crosses over the barricade. He strikes a Zameer Khan pose next to the hooded passenger and belts out dialogues with an energy that startles everybody.

An impromptu contest breaks out between the two. The security check of that small airport turns into an audition room, both the men trying to outdo each other with an eye on Sharman. The passengers join in, freely expressing their admiration and criticism. This last minute unexpected drama rounds up a good holiday for the departing sixteen, and augurs well for the incoming sixteen.

Sharman sinks on to a chair holding his head. The airport security manages to break up the drama by announcing the flight is ready for departure.

The grey hooded passenger, slings a rucksack over his shoulder and leaves. Within minutes the hall is empty. The emptiness multiplies Sharman's agitation. Secretary Honey sinks into an empty seat next to him, he is a genuinely worried man, 'I don't get it, he left without his phone...'

Sharman explodes, 'What the fuck do you know about him anyway? Must have gotten a new phone, a new secretary... You are a useless piece of shit! If I find out you've messed with me, sent him off to some other film shoot on my dates, I will fucking kill you.'

The death threat slides off Honey's thick hide, the 'new secretary' part unnerves him.

7

Standup

Late evening. Interior of the nightclub.

At the bar, near the far end of the lounge, behind a glass partition is Sharman. He is talking agitatedly with Secretary Honey. He gets a call. It is from an 'unknown' number.

'Hello.'

'Sup, bro?' Zameer Khan's voice filters through.

Sharman jumps out of his seat, 'Sup bro? Su...sup bro? You know damn well...'

Zameer's voice replies, with a characteristic drawl, 'What can I say man ...I'm fucking this hot babe...'

'Babe? I'm the one getting fucked here and you...'

Overlooking the bar is a lounge separated by a glass partition. In the lounge, on the small elevated stage, is the same passenger whom Samuel had mistaken for Zameer Khan. He is repeating his 'mimic Zameer' act. He is holding a mobile phone close to the microphone; it's on speaker mode. Sharman's voice is coming through loud and clear for the audience to hear.

The audience is in splits. Some are even pointing and turning to look at Sharman at the bar. The man lets out a few innovative curses, Sharman does the same on the other side. Without ever claiming to be Zameer, the man works Sharman into such a frenzy that he is frothing and fawning alternately, in irritation and confusion.

Abruptly, the man disconnects the call and switches his mobile phone off. On the other side of the partition, Sharman completely loses it and rushes out, dragging Honey with him. The crowd watches them rush out and breaks into applause.

The lounge manager introduces the man to the audience, 'And this is Vikram... Our guest performer for the night.'

Vikram takes a bow as the catcalls and claps fade away. Microphone in hand, he walks amongst the audience as he talks. Inviting comments and asking questions. He stops at a table, perches on top of the bar. The audience responds enthusiastically. Vikram has the natural ease of a veteran standup comic.

Rumana walks in with a bunch of girls. There is a kind of lethal moodiness in her expression. Some of her friends join in the exchange between Vikram and the audience.

'Hands up, all the women who would want to "disappear" with Zameer Khan,' Vikram says.

Nearly all the women hoot appreciatively and raise their hands. Rumana looks expressionless. She is the only one not laughing at her table.

A few feet away, Mahesh is at a table Vikram is leaning on, he notices Rumana's disdain. The sharp fear he felt, when she nearly bit his lip off, still rankles. 'Look at the bitch playing cool, last night she was ready to fuck me if I promised to get her close to Zameer. So fucking fickle.' Mahesh hisses.

Vikram registers the comment and Rumana. He continues his act, 'Hands up, all the men who would like to disappear with Zameer Khan!'

Giggles and guffaws.

He is moving towards the bar where Rumana is getting herself a drink. He notices her leave almost double the price of the drink on the bar and wander off. Arrogance or absent-mindedness, whatever it may be, it most definitely spells tons of money. He looks very interested. She is carrying a semi-transparent clutch and he can see the room key holder in it, he registers the room number. 698.

Vikram's act comes to an end, he gets applause and hoots in equal measure. He takes it all with an over the top bow. The live band takes over.

He looks around for Rumana, she is gone. He leaves the lounge in search of her. Outside, the night is silent and heavy with humidity. Wafts of smells from the meats being barbecued on the lawns interrupt his search. He feels his stomach growl. It's been many hours since he has eaten. But first, Rumana.

He catches sight of her. He observes her from a distance, allows her to see him and lets a bit of energy build up in the silent exchanges before he approaches her.

The manner and confidence with which he approaches her makes it clear that he is an expert with women, or at least he thinks he is. Maybe he is a conman who hangs around expensive resorts hoping to get lucky with some wealthy woman.

She still has a sulky look. Vikram makes his move.

'So you didn't think I was funny back there...'

'You are an actor?'

'No, a writer. Working with the script team for Zameer Khan's film. He'll be back, the shoot will start in a few days.'

She seems to be appraising him. Vikram seems pleased, it means the game is moving forward. He adds, 'Hey, that's what a star is supposed to do anyway! Act starry!'

Then her eyes go silent and she holds her inscrutable slit-eyed look for a long moment, as though deciding how to respond. He seems to be a rash victim literally pushing himself into the jaws of death. The thick cloud of indeterminate tension builds around them...

She blinks, the spell breaks. Then starts walking away. But Vikram is relentless, seems unaware of the palpable danger. He takes it as a game of 'playing hard to get'. He reaches out and slips his arm into hers.

'These four parts in the film I just wrote are up for casting. There is one that gets you real close to Zameer Khan.'

His message is very clear: I could swing it for you…if we do some swinging of our own before that.

'And just how close will it get me? Close enough to smell him…to touch him…'

She is wrapping herself around Vikram. He can't believe how easy this is. The menace in her eyes and the slight hissing of her voice seems to have eluded him completely.

'…to eat… '

Her tongue darts out in a sensual predatory manner reaching for his earlobe as she hisses each word out…he can feel her warm breath on his skin…the fragrance of her androgynous perfume… her teeth are about to sink into the soft skin…

Bang.

The door of the dance floor bursts open, noise and smoke spill out, along with a large group of energetic dancers caught in an euphoric mood. The crowd is jumping, dancing, singing and pushing. For a moment Rumana and Vikram are engulfed in the mass. Crushed even closer by the crowd. Vikram can feel the length of her body, taut and muscular. This is not a woman to trifle with.

Then almost like a wave that came in from the sea and ebbed back into it, the crowd moves on…takes Rumana with it. Vikram is left alone. The spell is broken.

Vikram is contemplating what to do next.

He makes his way through the sea-facing garden and reaches the exterior of a cottage. 698. The number on it is the same as the key in Rumana's transparent clutch.

The housekeeping staff is busy cleaning up inside the cottage. He studies the thrash that comes out. Booze bottles, a ripped up dress, broken makeup material, a small silver dessert spoon with its underside burnt. Everything screams 'party-girl'.

He waits till they leave. The door has a thumbprint identifier along with the lock. He ignores it and heads straight for the lock. He has it open in a few moments. A sensor concealed in the door records the door opening without the thumb identification.

Back at the hotel security room, a warning goes off, one of their surveillance cameras show a hazy video of a male figure as the door of room 698 closes.

Inside the room, Vikram is moving silently and rapidly. He is wearing gloves, scanning through the closets and drawers. He is picking stuff and putting it in a bag. He starts with the bedside tables, then the writing desk. Next, he moves to the chest of drawers in the dressing area behind a partition. The partition hides the room's entrance from his view.

Silently the door swings open and Rumana enters. She expected to find him inside. She sees his outline through the partition and starts moving towards him. Her feet move silently on the carpet. Her body is like a tightly coiled spring about to launch, she has a short knife in her left hand, concealed and ready to strike.

She is barely six feet away. He is still searching, looking around. She leaps ahead with blinding speed… But Vikram beats her to it. A fraction before her short knife makes contact, he swings around and tasers her.

His pen-shaped taser makes contact with her forearm and sends over twenty-six thousand volts racing through her. One… two…three…four…five seconds. The electro-muscular disruption triggered by the shock rides over her nervous system. The knife drops. She stumbles back and hits the bed first, then the wall. She slides to the floor and is twitching and shaking. Ignoring her completely, he calmly continues searching through her stuff.

There are loud sounds of boots running towards the room, the hotel security guards and the cops, Samuel and Roddy, burst in. They see Vikram. Samuel, with his newfound sense of importance, barks some incomprehensible contradicting orders at him. The only two words that can be made out are 'arrest' and 'police station'.

Silence.

Some weird mumbling noises fill the room. Rumana has still not recovered from her shock. She is gurgling and twitching behind the bed, out of sight. Samuel peeks and gets a shock seeing her wriggling body.

Vikram takes off his gloves and strides away purposefully. The cops are torn between chasing him and helping the girl. Vikram realizes he has walked out alone and peeps back into the room. He is back to his standup comedy act.

'I thought we are going to the police station?'

Everyone stands perplexed. Vikram marches off. Roddy dashes behind him. Samuel and the hotel security guard try to get Rumana on her feet. She is like jello, keeps slipping out of their hands.

Vikram asks Roddy, 'Did you take the evidence…? My bag…?'

Roddy has totally forgotten the bag, now he is stuck between leaving Vikram and returning to the room. So he yells.

'Sir! Sir!'

From inside the room, Samuel screams back, 'What an ass, why are you screaming?'

Rumana slips from Samuel's hands once more. He grabs her again and lifts.

'The bag, Sir, the evidence…just wanted to remind you, Sir,' Roddy yells back.

Samuel abuses him soundly and the aggression helps him to finally haul Rumana onto the bed. He and the guard step back, huffing and puffing from the exhaustion.

She sits up, the effect is dissipating. They are irritated. She wakes up now, after all the effort! Samuel barks orders for her to reach the police station immediately and leaves.

She remains sitting there dazed, Roddy races in, grabs the bag just as she is about to reach for it, and races out. She slips back into the bed.

A young woman peers into the room and sees the dishevelled Rumana on the bed.

'Hey, what happened? Are you sick...? Oh god, you are hurt, can I help you? I am in the next room... I heard...'

8

IG

A colonial stable converted into a police station. The board reads 'Police. Craig Island'.

It has a paid staff of three, and one volunteer. Samuel, Roddy and one peon who, right now, is sleeping in the far corner. The volunteer being Sir Fredrick (pronounced sar fedick), an overfed dusty brown mongrel, so-called for being born in Sir Fredrick Bradford's Guest House, before it was renamed as Rajiv Gandhi Vishram Ghar.

Sir Fredrick does a thorough job of sniffing every being that enters the police station. He lingers over Vikram's fingertips and crotch, till Vikram flicks his nose. Sir Fredrick sneezes, showering droplets of doggy snot on Vikram's pants, then retires into the yard.

Samuel is trying to get it right by declaring Vikram's arrest formally. He demands a photo ID. Vikram presents one, it's not a photo ID, it's a laminated visiting card. Samuel reads it.

'Jai Mahakali Taxi Service. All tipe kar supplier, relable drvers, contact Hari Chaurasia, Bandipur... You are Hari Chaurasia!'

Vikram hands over another card, 'My mistake.'

Samuel reads aloud, 'Ek Minar cable operator, Moishin Anwar Umerruddin Khetriwale Sheikh...what kind of a...'

Vikram grabs the card back apologizing profusely, 'Shit! Sorry... Here, here.' He hands over a laminated ID.

By now Samuel has lost interest and passes it on to Roddy, who starts blindly filling up the arrest form on the computer. He types with one finger, searching for letters on the keyboard. It's obvious that not much happens around here.

Meanwhile, Vikram has marched into the inner office as though it's the perfectly natural thing for a recently arrested burglar to do.

Roddy mutters as he types, 'Name, Vikram…'

Clang! clash… thud…

Vikram is standing next to a table with many of its recent contents scattered on the floor. Samuel races in. Vikram is looking around, smiling innocently as though he had nothing to do with the items that now find themselves on the floor. Samuel is searching for the right words to admonish this insolent burglar when Roddy calls out loudly.

'Surname…Singh Shekhavat…why does he have two surnames…occupation, IG…IG? Sir, what kind of an occupation is IG…'

Samuel rushes out and grabs the card again, few more sounds come from the room, including a plastic chair that comes flying out. Samuel is about to explode when the meaning of the word IG dawns on him. He deflates.

Inside, Vikram, with one sweep of the arm, finally manages to empty the entire paraphernalia from the table.

Samuel wails, 'Oh shit! IG Police Vikram Singh Shekhawat, you idiot. He is an IPS officer.' He winces as some more sounds come from inside his ex-office room.

As Samuel and Roddy haltingly re-enter, Vikram sits on Samuel's chair (former), puts his legs on Samuel's table (former) and smiles brightly at them. He utters a single command, 'Tea.'

Both rush out to comply.

Rumana, accompanied by the helpful next-door neighbour, enters the police station, she grabs Samuel, 'That man, he tasered me, you have to arrest him immediately…'

Samuel pries himself out of her fingers and rushes for tea. Rumana rushes into the inner office, fully expecting to meet the higher officer. She comes to a grinding halt when she sees Vikram. Something inside her snaps and she lunges straight over the desk to grab him. To her surprise, the helpful neighbour grabs her by her waist belt and holds her back. She struggles to be released and screams abuses at Vikram.

'You are arrested for attempting to cause bodily harm to an officer and thereby obstructing him in the due performance of his duty etc… etc… Tashi, lock her up.'

Tashi, the 'helpful neighbour' replies with a resounding voice, 'Yes, Sir!'

With a sudden burst of added force, Tashi half drags, half pushes Rumana to the lock-up. Rumana is stunned as it dawns on her that Vikram is a cop and so is this woman.

Clang! Tashi shuts the lock-up door. But there is only a latch, no lock! Rumana realizes it and starts clawing at Tashi. Roddy hurriedly rummages for the lock and key in his desk.

Four men enter the police station. It's the two beach boys, Mahesh, and the owner of the fishing trawler. They eye Rumana from a distance. They are led by a young overly groomed officer, Ranbeer Khurana.

Beach boy 1 points at Rumana, 'Yes, Sir, that's her. Six… six-fifteen in the morning at the waterfront. She went off in the boat. Alone.'

'Are you sure? Look again.' Vikram asks.

Beach boy 2 chuckles, 'We've had a close look at her a few nights ago. I mean, yes, it's her, she was in a blue dress…'

'She is nuts, she bit me man, would have ripped it off…' Mahesh adds.

All the men involuntarily look towards his crotch in alarm.

'... My lip, man! My lip...look...'

Nobody is interested.

'What's she done now?'

Roddy replies, 'Attacked an officer on duty.'

'Bound to happen.'

The fisherman adds his story, 'Yes, yes, she was wearing a blue dress when I saw her, around eight-thirty in the morning I think. Was coming from the direction of the island...'

Rumana has heard part of their statements and is shouting, 'Bullshit! Lies, lies...it wasn't me, it wasn't...I can prove it... I can.'

The men are hustled into the verandah by Samuel. Tashi gets busy taking down their statements. Small-town boy Roddy is staring at Rumana as though she is some exotic animal.

Vikram's mobile phone vibrates indicating a call. On its screen, an icon shows an animated frog gobbling flies with its long tongue. He watches it for a few moments, letting the mobile ring, then answers, almost gloating.

'Prime suspect Rumana Dhawan identified and arrested. Witnesses' statements being taken.'

Heavy silence on the other end.

At the other end is Deputy Director General of Police Raghavender Harishchandra Bansal. He is Vikram's senior officer and does have an uncanny resemblance to the cartoon frog.

Raghav is in his office, behind a huge table with his name and designation written on a small plaque. He is chewing his lip, digesting the information, he might as well have been the frog licking the juices of the recently gobbled fly. He doesn't look too happy about Vikram's report. Snorts.

Click. Vikram has reported and unceremoniously disconnected.

9

Twisted

Twelve hours ago.
Mumbai. India.

A 2D manga cartoon with a dreamish quality. A young frightened Japanese girl in a school uniform is being chased by Japanese goons. Squealing helplessly in Japanese, she stumbles and turns around a corner. She catches sight of a dumpster. Dives behind it.

Suddenly, there is a blinding flash of light. Her clothes explode in slo mo. As they explode they turn into shreds barely covering her body. An overtly sexual superwoman costume appears on her. She is no cowering schoolgirl. She is a superheroine in disguise.

The goons catch up and get the shock of their lives when they see this woman radiating brilliant light, flashing tits and muscles at the same time.

A samurai sword appears in her hands, she utters a string of war cries in Japanese and proceeds to thrash the goons mercilessly. They go flying off in different directions with comic horror on their face. She violently thrusts her sword forward as though stabbing the bad guys continuously.

Somewhere along the way, the 2D superwoman character and samurai sword start transforming and the Japanese war cries change.

Transformation complete, she has morphed into a large swarthy bearded bear-like man, Dr Anand. The sword has transformed into a disproportionately large toothbrush frothing with toothpaste. It is pointed straight into something. It's swinging in and out, Anand is brushing the teeth of some person who is lying down.

Mumbles, groans and the toothpaste splatters on Anand, spat out by the victim of this forced oral hygiene exercise.

It's Vikram, he is lying pinned down on a bed. The bear-like Anand is sitting astride him, brushing his teeth forcibly.

'This is not what I signed up for when I let you move in. Wake up, you dog. You've been out for two whole days…'

The violently struggling Vikram, appalled by Anand, finally heaves hard enough and manages to dislodge him. 'How many fucking times have I told you not to do that…'

Anand guffaws unrepentant. Vikram sights another man in the room, 'Who the fuck are you?'

The smooth-faced dapper-looking young man, replies with a sense of importance, 'Ranbeer Khurana. Deputy DGP Raghavender Harishchandra Bansal sent me. You have to report to him in thirty-two minutes.'

Vikram's face darkens with anger, he continues to curse under his breath as he enters the bathroom and bangs the door close.

Anand spies something sticking out from under the bed cover. It's lacy underwear. He lifts it with the end of a clothes hanger and yells, 'How many times have I told you not to get random whores into my house.'

'She was not a whore.'

'What type of woman fails to notice an underwear missing when she walks out of the door… Or, maybe you were wearing it!'

He guffaws so wickedly that Vikram opens the door and sends a mug full of water in his direction. Khurana looks on a bit confused at this 'boy's dorm' antics of the two grown-up men. It's tough to maintain the sharp self-important air in this ruckus.

Thirty-five minutes later. Crime branch HQ. Interior.

Vikram stares wide-eyed as the reflection of the film he is watching flickers on his face. The two-minute film shows Zameer Khan's snuff killing, as uploaded by the killer. Then he grins from ear to ear, 'Box office hit!'

Deputy DGP Raghavender Harishchandra Bansal is not amused. Vikram has always been a good means of testing his anger management skills. Tashi switches off the miniature projector and settles down to watch the fun.

'He is known to have been missing from around the time this surfaced on a snuff porn website.' Raghav says.

'That means it happened…it's not a gimmick, film promo…? Not computer graphic or something…'

Raghav glares at him wordlessly.

Vikram asks, 'She just killed him on camera…and posted it?'

'… and probably made tons of money,' Raghav mutters.

'That's so fucking cool!' Vikram interjects.

Raghav inhales to curb his irritation, gestures at Tashi to continue.

'It happened in the last four hours, on an island off Lakshadweep. That's where he spent the night,' she replays a portion of the film. 'Check out the position of the sun and the path of the flight overhead. That's the BA 658 on its scheduled flight path right above the island. So this… happened around seven this morning. He was last seen around six-thirty this morning by his girlfriend, Shilpa.'

Vikram asks, 'About the website, any track on it?'

'None,' replies Raghav. 'It vanished even as the final frame of the film played out.'

'I don't understand…'

'In all likelihood, it's spot subscribed, possibly by an exclusive international group of jaded rich men and women, who can no longer get it off unless they see something truly insane. Sex, violence and death of a man as famous as Zameer Khan.'

'So, which dirty old man passed this on to you?'

'That's strictly outside the purview of your assignment.'

'Eighteen months of disciplinary desk work and you bring me out for this? Why couldn't it have been a jealous husband killing his wife.'

Raghav takes a dig, 'You are our resident porn expert!'

Vikram snaps back, 'What do you expect me to do for nine hours a day in an empty office where nothing happens?'

Raghav smirks, 'It's showing up on your annual review. Gross misuse of security clearance status to browse banned and objectionable Internet data. Enough to guarantee a suspension order. Get this right and we may mark it as...research.'

'I know why you are unloading this shit on me, you've got your fall guy in place even before the case starts!'

'Na, I got you in because only a twisted mind can get to the bottom of this twisted act.'

'Thanks, chief, I am sure you mean it as a compliment.'

Tashi, with a barely concealed smile, watches the men go back and forth.

Raghav instructs, 'As of now, the crime will remain under wrap. Local cops were informed but no missing report has been filed. We will make the announcement when we are ready. Khurana will be joining you.'

It's clear that Khurana is going to be Raghav's watchdog over them. Vikram's distaste is barely concealed as they walk out. Tashi's look says this is going to be fun, this head-banging between the rams. There is also an unmistakable look of pity for Khurana.

Tashi is the fifth child of a Tibetan father and a Punjabi

mother, five feet ten in her socks with a reed-like slimness and a razor-sharp mind. With four elder brothers to contend with, men hold no mysteries for her.

10
Alibi

Back to the present. Late night. In the police station at Craig Island.

In the outer room, fight master Roger is seated across the table from Tashi. He eyes Rumana with that special distaste that men reserve for women who make them feel overwhelmed. It's a look that Tashi knows only too well, she too has been at the receiving end more times than she cares to recollect. She finds him boring and predictable, a chore to be completed quickly and efficiently. He is full of information, 'Booked for attacking the officer? Had to happen. She has been nothing but trouble.'

'Then why did you give her the assignment?' Tashi asks.

'Let me tell you, she is super fit and well trained. No doubt, she was better and faster at the stunt than any of my other men. But irregulars like her, always create problems…'

Next, Tashi grills Samuel, 'What about the ferry service to the island?'

'Three times a week,' he tells her.

'When did the last one take passengers?'

'The evening before he disappeared.'

'When is the next one?'

'Tomorrow morning.'

'Do they have video surveillance at the wharf?'

'Yes.'

Tashi is surprised, 'What are you waiting for? Go get the

footage, hey, wait... what about private boats? They can come and go as they please?'

Samuel shrugs, 'Yes, only rich folk own them...so...'

Inside the office, Vikram gets another call. It's Khurana. 'I think we have a problem...about Rumana's alibi for the time of the killing,' he says.

Vikram frowns.

Khurana is at the hotel's security console. He has pulled out and lined up the surveillance footage from the night before. Four television sets reveal the feed from four different closed-circuit cameras. The videos have a clock count at the bottom, showing the exact time they were recorded.

2:00 a.m., 4:00 a.m., 5:30 a.m. ...sure enough, Rumana was on the dance floor through the night leading up to Zameer's disappearance. She is always in the company of her friends.

Khurana holds up his mobilephone so that Vikram can watch each video as it plays out.

Vikram watches the videos on his mobile phone. Sounds from the nightclub and crowds filter through.

Rumana is still protesting loudly from inside the lock-up, 'I was dancing all night at the hotel. The club played the last number at six in the morning, my request, go check it out. I had breakfast at seven, in the coffee shop. Get me out of here. I demand... I...'

On the surveillance tapes at 5:15 a.m., she leaves the dance floor with a man. She disappears with him behind some bushes. It's obvious that she and the man were making out. Some of her friends wander out for a breather.

The footage shows one friend discover Rumana and immediately call everybody to take a look. They hoot and cheer. The man staggers out, outraged at the aggressive women. Rumana walks out giggling.

Khurana declares, 'I'm heading to interview the nightclub staff…'

Vikram, pensive, waits. Khurana finds the DJ sleeping in a cubbyhole behind the music console. 'Ya, the closing number was her request, around six I guess…,' the DJ says.

Next in line is the waiter in the coffee shop, 'Breakfast opens at seven, table number 23, Ms Dhawan plus three were there… they served themselves from the buffet, they left at eight, eight thirty I guess…'

Vikram has watched the interviews live. Khurana turns the camera off and speaks to Vikram, 'Looks like it couldn't have been her…'

'Talk to her friends,' Vikram instructs him.

Khurana does as he is told. He finds a gang of young women around the pool, stretched out in various states of disarray, like the leftovers of a wild party. The same women who had hooted and cheered watching Rumana make out with the man behind the bushes.

A fake blonde with deep brown Indian skin squints as she hears Khurana's questions. Then replies, 'Of course, she was with us.' She continues squinting at him, should she fuck him or…? Na, too much effort. She sinks back into the soft darkness she had surfaced from.

Khurana, momentarily flattered by her overt evaluation, walks away slowly deliberating on a life of perpetual holiday. On his way out he picks up a brochure on the spa. Vampire facial, it screams. He immediately puts it down, it was not for him; he would stick to his monthly banana–strawberry mix.

Back at the police station, after the interviews, Khurana summarizes the investigation for Vikram. 'The coffee shop footage of her wipes out the testimony of all the witnesses. The beach boys who say they saw her at the jetty around six and the fishing trawler owner's claims of having seen around eight at sea.'

Khurana is waiting for Vikram to give an order to release Rumana. But something is gnawing Vikram. He does not want to let her go.

He says, 'She had a motive…'

Rumana has kept up a tireless harangue from inside the lock-up. She is now threatening legal action.

Tashi and Roddy walk in. Sir Fredrick dutifully sniffs them and immediately goes into a sneezing fit. Roddy is triumphantly holding up a small pouch. It's marijuana. They found it in her room.

Vikram's mood lightens.

The cops add 'marijuana possession' to the 'assault on police officer' case that has been registered against her.

Rumana insists, 'That's not mine, it wasn't in my room. It couldn't have been. No. No…'

Vikram watches as her aggression shifts to defence, she has forgotten her threats of legal action against Vikram and is completely focused on defending herself from the drug accusation.

Vikram calls, 'Hey, Samuel.' Samuel, who had been banished to the outside corridor rushes in. 'Make out the papers for the magistrate, at least a week in custody. Tashi, do your stuff.'

Tashi is equipped with one of the best forensic field kits in the country. It had been her most treasured possession for over a month now. As a top field forensics expert, she had been assigned the job of testing its efficiency, before a bunch of paper pushers, haggled, collected commissions and placed an order for the department.

Rumana refuses to cooperate. Surprisingly, Tashi doesn't need her to. First, she holds up a face mapper that, within seconds, records every contour of Rumana's face and neck from ear to ear.

Then she uses the same scanner to scan and record her body contours. It's done within moments even before Rumana realizes it.

Finally, Tashi uses a tweezer to pick a sliver of broken nail that Rumana has just bitten off in anxiety and spat out onto the floor.

Sample sealed and packed, she is ready to move. Rumana is sulking in her cell. But a darker light is filling up her eyes now.

Khurana says to Tashi, 'Does Vikram know she is Rumana Dhawan? Daughter of Rakesh Dhawan, the hotel magnet?'

'You think he doesn't?'

'He entered her room without a warrant then tasered her! Fucking tasered her! Who does that? Why was he even carrying a taser! The "assault on an officer" was not going to stick. Her father would have taken his arse if not for that lucky marijuana find.'

Tashi, within Vikram's earshot, says, 'He always plays it too close, and not always with his own arse.'

Vikram laughs, 'The marijuana will hold her back on the island for a bit, we may need her.'

Khurana suddenly gets suspicious, he whispers to Tashi, 'Shit! She is telling the truth...he placed it in her room. Where did he get it?'

Tashi is really irritated now, seems like she has to spoon-feed him everything.

'Go really close and smell...'

He does. Barely discernable whiffs of the marijuana cling to Vikram, sometime during the night, Vikram smoked it. That means the marijuana belonged to Vikram, not Rumana!

Khurana hurriedly moves away to make a call, presumably to Raghav. Vikram notices it.

It's near dawn. The three of them are already heading out to an unmarked battered-looking seaplane.

'I could get used to it, Raghav is really spreading it out for us.' Tashi says.

'Zameer had nearly two thousand crores riding on him in the next three years,' says Khurana.

'Too bad his best performance will never make it to the Oscars. Want to bet? She will be on the phone with daddy before we get on that plane,' says Vikram.

11

Talk to Me

The tiny noisy plane circles the island searching for the spot they saw in the film. The villa is visible at one end along with the path leading to the jetty. The other end has undisturbed foliage and sandy clearings. Tashi matches the still frames from the film to the topography. They locate the sand bar. Time to take a closer look. Khurana keeps clicking away, covering every approach to the clearing.

They are now on the beach at the exact spot of the killing. It's 6:45 a.m., almost the same time as yesterday when the killing happened. The flight they saw in the film passes overhead again. It's a mere speck in the sky, but a significant speck that had made its way into the killer's 6K cameras the day before.

Vikram is perched on a rock, staring intently at the sand where Zameer lay twenty-four hours ago. He studies the different shots in the film and works backwards, locating the position of each camera. Two on the palm trees...two in the undergrowth. The sand around the possible locations is undisturbed. The trunks of the trees are unmarked. No visible clue.

Tashi marks the area where Zameer lay. She unloads her kit and gets to work rapidly with Khurana's help. The tide is not fully in and the sand is exposed. She knows she probably has just minutes before the tide reaches the spot. She sprays luminol on the sand, puts on her wrap around wide spectrum glasses and waits.

She waits for the luminol to act with the iron from any

blood traces that may be present in the sand. The blood flow from Zameer's torn neck had been substantial. Some of it should still be present.

No luminescent iron stains in the sand, there is no blood splatter here. Tashi is surprised, she tries again, shrugs.

'Nothing here...,' she calls out.

'All washed away by the waves?' Khurana asks.

'Not possible,' she replies.

'Superb professional cleanup?' Vikram inquires.

Tashi nods. She doesn't like it. Forensics needs criminals to make mistakes, leave traces.

Exactly at the spot where Zameer's neck lay, she digs three inches into the sand and rapidly sprays the luminol again. The blood could have soaked in and traces may have remained unwashed.

The result is negative. The waves have reached the spot, she has probably a minute before the hole fills up with the saltwater. She is puzzled, not defeated. She jabs a large-mouth syringe into the sand and pulls out the sand from three inches under the surface. She collects it in a sterilized pouch. Working swiftly, she jabs in another place. By the time the water covers the spot, she has collected four different samples of sand from under the surface.

Vikram makes a call to Raghav. He is not happy at having to retreat. 'I need the full film, the way it was given to you. It needs more investigation.'

Raghav gloats, 'I thought it was a closed case already?' He hangs up.

Vikram mulls, 'The whole setup... It had to be precise... rehearsed...'

'It had to be timed to the tide...' Tashi adds.

'They have left us nothing...' Khurana says.

'There is always something...' Vikram knows better.

Vikram lies down on the now wet spot where Zameer's body was and tries to get into the mind of the dying filmstar.

He can see the sky above, the circling gulls. The small waves keep brushing around him with increasing intensity. Khurana watches him, bemused.

Vikram mutters, 'What did you see? ...what did you see...?' He seems to be asking the birds... he seems to be asking Zameer... Flashes of the killer, from Zameer's point of view, run through Vikram's mind. It's a point of view never revealed by the uploaded film. Vikram's mind is feverishly trying to recreate it. He is unconcerned of the waves rising up his cheeks now.

He imagines the killer sitting astride him, her hands making patterns on his torso, the sharp jabs and the accompanying pain that showed on Zameer's face. She was wearing one camera on her body...that's what had shown the details of the fingers jabbing into the neck, the artery spurting blood. The bitch was super prepared.

Then he sees it, to his right, ten feet away, the rocks end. There is a clear circular depression, just an inch long, close-set against the rock. Behind it is a natural break in the thorny bushes, almost like a path.

He gets up dripping water, drenched from head to toe. Makes his way to the print.

He imagines in his mind's eye that Zameer and the killer must have come through this path over the stones. The depression could be Zameer's bare heel landing hard into the sand. By some quirk, the waves didn't reach here.

They study the aerial pictures taken by Khurana, yes, the path extended all the way to the lagoon, partially separating it from the island as the tide rose.

Tashi and Khurana enact the entry of Zameer and the killer

through the narrow path. Vikram finds some broken thorns on a bush. Tashi sprays it with luminol. Within moments she can clearly see minuscule specs of lit material. She is looking at skin scrapings with minuscule quantity of blood trapped in it. Finally, something tangible. Could be either Zameer's or the killer's, it's a stroke of luck. If this matches Rumana's, they could nail her. They start fine-combing the area and discover another clue, a single strand of long burgundy-coloured hair. The colour matches the killer's hair in the film and Rumana's hair. Tashi puts it in a sanitized plastic pouch.

The three of them trudge across the sand to the villa. It's empty and undisturbed. A quick search reveals nothing suspicious. Tashi collects the razor and toothbrush for Zameer's DNA samples.

12

Pancakes

Back on the mainland. A small beach-side shack. Vikram, still wearing his damp clothes, is wolfing down his breakfast. A large pancake with dollops of cream and chocolate sauce. Tashi is eyeing it with disdain, drinking black coffee and nibbling from a bowl of cut papaya. Khurana is at a distance, on the mobile phone, presumably reporting to Raghav once again.

Vikram gets a call. It's Shekhar from the cyber team.

Shekhar is staring at the snuff film playing in a loop on his monitor. 'Nothing to report, Sir. The film clip holds no information of its source or its travel till it reached Raghav's mail.'

Vikram asks, 'How can that be? Some server info? IP address? A payment gateway? A lot of money was paid by folks who saw it. There has to be some connection to some bank, some credit card...'

'What we have is a screen recording of the original file, not a copy,' says Shekhar. 'You need to get to the source from where this screen recording was made.'

Vikram goes back to his breakfast. Too much hinges on the hair and bloodstain they found. Even if the hair matches Rumana's, it would not be enough to prove her guilt. All it would prove is that she had been on the island. Her lawyers and she would certainly have the best her daddy could buy, would reduce it to 'inconclusive circumstantial evidence'.

Three words he intensely disliked. He had heard them too

many times.

As he mulls over things, he notices a rather largish teenaged boy, seated on the other side of the restaurant. The boy observes what Vikram is eating, discusses with the waiter and orders the same.

Sharman plonks himself in the chair opposite Vikram, his face is haggard, eyes bloodshot. His hair is more spikey than usual.

Sharman asks, 'Is it true? Have you seen it?'

Vikram pretends Sharman does not exist. Sharman persists, 'Look, I need to know, I've got fucking three hundred crores riding on Zameer. This film is half done, the last one…the less said the better… I am dead!'

Vikram orders a hot chocolate. Sharman ignores Vikram's lack of interest in him and continues, 'Before the news gets into the market, I'm gonna sell my film's rights to whoever buys it and recover at least a part of my money.'

Vikram is still silent. When he overhears a voice order a hot chocolate, he looks up to find the same young man ordering it. He continues attacking his pancake. Sharman is now watching Vikram with the heavy hooded eyes of a vulture.

Sharman continues talking, 'Actually, I have a terrific idea, we are going to do this as a joint venture. Who has the rights to Zameer's snuff film? I am told its red smoking hot. I want to buy that. Find the owner and lock it for me. I tell you, we will make a killing with it.'

For the first time, Vikram looks Sharman in the eye, he is stumped by the unexpected offer. Sharman places his business card on the table and walks out.

Tashi gets a call; it's Samuel. 'It's confirmed, Madam, only one private boat went out that morning, the one that belongs to the resort. The one that the beach-boys claimed Rumana went on. Six fishing trawlers went out, the usual fishing teams, they all came back.'

'So, no one else could have left this island by sea?'

'Seems like that, Madam.'

'And what about the plane that took us to the island this morning?'

'Yours was the first trip he made in a week.'

Khurana has returned to the table.

Tashi turns to Vikram, 'We need satellite images for the period, just to make sure there really was no movement by sea or air from Zameer's island villa.'

13

Butt on Fire

Mumbai. Four days since Zameer's death.

Interior of Raghav's office. The entire team is assembled for a debriefing. Tashi has an update, 'The skin cells we found on the island match Zameer's, but the hair does not match Rumana's DNA.'

Disappointing, but not unexpected. Vikram shrugs, 'Zameer made out with a different woman every day. A dozen different girls could have been on the island with him. That hair could be anybody's.'

The intercom lights up.

Raghav's secretary is on the line, 'Sirji, the DG's office again, they are waiting…'

Raghav disconnects without giving a reply. His jowls are quivering in suppressed agitation.

He informs the team, 'You have to let Rumana go immediately. Her father is sitting with the director general right now. She is a Canadian citizen, her Embassy has already asked for an explanation. The assault on a police officer on duty, it's not going to stick on her. And Zameer's killing is still not registered as an offence, so she can't be booked as a suspect for it.'

Tashi opens another envelope, reads from it, 'She does have traces of cocaine in her nail clipping.'

'Bingo!' exclaims Vikram. 'That's all we need. That's what you are going to tell the DG. She stays.'

Raghav looks crestfallen. These kids of the rich and mighty are always bad news.

Vikram continues, 'She had clear motives! Remember, she came there with the precise motive of fucking him. She went through a whole lot of planning and effort to have action master Roger get her close to Zameer.'

Raghav mutters, 'I don't get this woman, she moves in a society where she could have simply got herself introduced to him...at a party...a club...'

'Too easy. She is a predator by instinct, she doesn't think much about men who come easy,' says Vikram.

'But why would she want to be a stunt double?' Tashi asks.

'She wanted to meet him not as a bimbo groupie but as an equal. She is determined and unpredictable.'

The intercom rings again. Raghav doesn't bother answering it, he swiftly gets up to leave for the DG's office. The stress on him is palpable. Khurana is out of his chair in a flash, holding the door open for Raghav. Vikram gets up and faces Raghav squarely, 'I know your butt is on fire, let the fat burn a bit longer. This murder is the first in a completely new generation of crime. Trust me, this could be just the beginning. It's gonna take you places you never imagined.'

Then Vikram dramatically leaves, closing the door smartly behind him. Khurana, in his current status of a doorman, opens the door once again and this time Raghav exits. As Raghav marches out, he is accosted by Sharman, who falls in step with him.

'Sirji, did you think about the offer for the murder film rights? Just five minutes of your time, Sir?' he says in a hushed tone.

Raghav keeps marching. Sharman drops off. This is obviously the wrong time. In the meantime, he spies Khurana coming out of Raghav's office, makes a beeline for him.

14

Pixel

A large hall, empty of all furniture except four chairs. Vikram is in the centre. An entire wall, nearly twenty feet by twenty feet has been converted into a projection screen. Vikram is playing the film over and over again. At that giant size, the impact is stunning.

He doesn't know what he is searching for. By now, even Khurana is stifling a yawn. He decides to amuse himself by placing himself directly behind Vikram and observing his shaved head very closely. Vikram feels the stare at the back of his head, turns around and catches Khurana at it. 'What do you see?' he asks.

Khurana is speechless. He mistakes Vikram's question to be about his bald head.

'Strength, sexuality, confidence…' responds Tashi.

Vikram nods, 'Yes, it's a woman's ultimate position of power, over life and death. What else…planning, precision, knowledge…'

'Strategy…' Khurana adds.

'Strategy to lure him in…strategy to use the dark web… strategy to upload the film…strategy to collect money for it…' says Vikram.

'Strategy to reach and gather beforehand viewers who would be interested… And who would pay,' says Tashi.

Vikram is thoughtful, 'This didn't happen on a whim. It was meticulously planned, she was supposed to be seen, yet never identified.'

Khurana is almost preening, Vikram's expansion of his one

word 'strategy' is making him feel quite bright. Vikram falls silent, goes back to playing and replaying the film.

Khurana slides his chair across the room to Tashi, 'Why does he shave?'

Tashi ignores him.

'I mean, he has a headful of hair, I observed the stubble very closely, he has...a lot of hair. Men like their hair...'

'Why didn't you ask him? By the way Khurana, why do you shave?'

Khurana is mighty pleased, grins from ear to ear, he does have superbly clean-shaven chest and arms. Tashi suddenly realizes that he has interpreted her observation as 'female interest'. He gives her what he considers a hot look. She winces; the man is a prize ass.

Involuntarily, her attention shifts to Vikram. His body has gone rigid, neck stretched. He has frozen a frame and zoomed in onto something. He is now standing barely a few feet away from the screen, staring at it. She walks over.

'What?' she asks.

'I saw...felt something...'

He flicks a few frames back, then forward. Tashi is staring at the screen too, she can't see anything she has not seen before. He plays it again. Then freezes a frame. It was just after the killer has hit Zameer in the heart area and Zameer's eyes have misted up with the sharp pain. The unshed tear is still just a film on his eyeball. For just a fraction, that film on the eyeball turns into a reflective surface. That's what had caught Vikram's attention.

Vikram remembers, as he lay in the exact spot where Zameer was killed, the killer rose against the sky like a nemesis and the gulls above.

There is something showing up on the reflective watery surface in Zameer's eyes. Vikram's pupils dilate to focus sharply on the image, adrenaline pumps through him as though in a physical chase. The artery on his right temple, at the edge of his shaved hairline, is throbbing slightly. His mouth has run dry, his throat is constricted.

He can see it clearly now, even though others can't. He is staring at it as though mesmerized.

15

Wall of Possibilities

Shekhar and team have set up their workstations in the screening room. The frames from the film that Vikram had been staring at have been isolated and magnified a hundred times.

There are ten frames with fractions of what looks like a face reflected on the victim's tear-film-covered eyeballs. Pixel by pixel, painstakingly the digital artists attach them and create a face spread. A portion of the right profile, a bit of the left, some of the chin area. But there are many gaps for which they don't have anything.

Vikram is edgy and pacing around them, bearing down on them with his characteristic impatience. The large screen shows their tedious progress.

Shekhar mutters, 'Hey buddy, why don't you take a break? This could take a while.'

Vikram realizes he is being politely told to leave. Shekhar is right, they can't move any faster. Mirroring what they have, the artists have to digitally reconstruct the possible face. 'Call me the moment you are ready,' he instructs as he leaves.

Vikram heads across the street to a small restaurant. Takes the innermost table with his back to the door. He is blocking out everything, wanting to focus on what he saw.

He orders a triple-decker sandwich with lemonade. He imagines a face forming on the dark wall in front of him.

He is about to take a bite of his sandwich when he hears a voice.

'Triple-decker sandwich and lemonade.'

Turning back he sees the same boy from the island. He is once again ordering what Vikram is eating. Why is this kid following him? Which part of his fucked up past has the kid crawled out from?

Vikram studies him as he munches his sandwiches. The young boy seems to be in his late teens. His British accent and diction reveal an upper-class education. Yet, he is dressed in depressing run-down grunge.

Vikram's mobile phone vibrates. 'Done,' says a text from Shekhar. He drops money on the table, forgets the boy and rushes out.

He walks into the screening room and is confronted with the twenty-feet-high re-constructed face. A supremely striking, frighteningly mesmeric face. The sunlight behind her head has created a bloody halo around her burgundy hair. He feels every muscle in his body go instantly taut, his breath catch.

It's a face he has never seen in his life…

…Yet, it feels like he recognizes it.

The only thing that is in the shadows is her eyes. The angle of her head has created a natural shade. This is the face that Zameer watched as he died. Vikram has pried out the secret, the killer worked so hard to conceal. It is the face that took over from Rumana for the killing.

He stays there for a long time, staring at the screen. Still searching…for what? He does not know. But he does know that he will have no rest till he looks into those eyes.

He is brought back to reality when Tashi taps him on the

shoulder, 'I have sent the pictures to the island. They will search airport and ferry records, hotels, nightclubs…surveillance cameras from every place Zameer visited and could have met the killer…'

It's now forty-eight hours since the face came up.

The island check comes up with nothing.

All public records are being scanned. Passport, college, university student data, voter's ID data, Facebook, Instagram and a dozen other social networking sites and image galleries are being checked. No match so far.

Vikram is feverish with impatience. He is staring at the face for the hundredth time, he can still feel the tingle at the back of his neck.

Tashi walks into Vikram's office with a printout, places it on the table. It's a driver's licence issued by the Parivahan Seva Mumbai office. 'It's a far cry from the image in Zameer's eye, but it's the nearest thing the facial recognition software has thrown up. There is a name and an address,' she tells him.

Tashi is right, the woman in the photo is a far cry from the mesmeric face they are searching. Her image is flat and bland, hair pulled back, startled eyes with deep dark circles. Vikram's wild woman looks worse than a dowdy housewife, he sighs.

The name is Dr Nicole Augusto, holds Portuguese citizenship. Currently living in Mumbai.

'We have to find her,' says Vikram. 'Then find the evidence to arrest her…or get her to confess. Check if there is a connection between Nicole and Rumana. Remember, there is still no offence registered about Zameer's murder. So, officially, this is not happening till the killer is nailed or the DG's office decides to let it become public.'

'But why aren't they registering the case? He is dead for sure, murdered for sure, what's the big deal?' Khurana wants to know.

Tashi shrugs, 'We are mere mortals following orders...'

Vikram is frustrated, 'The source! They are protecting the fucking source from where that film came. They will declare Zameer murdered only after we get the killer and the case can be suitably dressed to do away with the need to disclose the source.'

Khurana walks away nodding, suitably enlightened.

16

Watching You

The surveillance team swings into action. They get her as she leaves her home in the morning. It's always in a cab booked just minutes in advance, never in her sedan parked in the building garage.

At nine in the morning, she reaches a small NGO where she handles the SOS suicide line along with two other volunteers. In between her calls, she catches up with a stream of visitors. Women, young girls and boys meet her for counselling in the airy sunlit room.

Khurana tries calling the SOS number several times hoping to get her on the line. Each time, he lands up with the well-meaning retired army major who probably frightens the callers into giving up all thoughts of suicide by commanding them not to.

Tashi tries her luck, Nicole answers.

Tashi freezes, what the fuck should she say? She has never been suicidal.

'I have been thinking of suicide a lot lately.'

'We all do at some time or the other, life can get pretty rough.'

'I think I am going to kill myself...'

'You are having a bad day, why don't you go out and hang out with your buddies for a bit, you will feel better. If not, give me a call again same time tomorrow.'

'Ya, ok. Right.'

Hangs up.

Khurana is sneering at her, 'That was so darn lame. She saw right through you.' Tashi knows he is right. But that also proves that Nicole is a very sharp person.

At one in the afternoon, Nicole leaves the NGO, picks up a sandwich from a nearby Subway, where she is a regular. She sits in a park and munches carefully.

Tashi reports back, 'She is the only person I know who actually chews each bite thirty times before swallowing!'

'That comes from discipline or intimate knowledge of extreme hunger...' says Vikram.

Then a coffee from Starbucks. She continues her walk, gazing at shop windows, or browsing through a street bookstall. Nicole discards the empty coffee cup in a trashcan. Tashi moves in to get the cup for DNA analysis. She looks into the thrash and finds ten Starbucks coffee cups, which one was Nicole's?

Then starts the second part of Nicole's day in a bigger, more-swanky corporate psychiatric department.

Tashi reports back to Vikram, 'Six to eight patients daily. Thirty to forty minutes each. Mostly teenagers, some women and an occasional man. She sees everyone out to the reception. The younger ones instinctively hug her.'

Khurana adds, 'She leaves at 6:30 p.m. Takes a cab back home. Later in the evening, she jogs in the park with her pugs.'

Khurana plays a video on his mobile, 'That's her, stopping for the second time in ten minutes to catch her breath. Hardly the sign of the super-fit body that banged the life out of Zameer Khan.'

Vikram is pensive, the profile so far doesn't show any indication of homicidal tendencies, but...human beings are a mystery, women more so.

Tashi reports, 'Her building security camera shows her taking the dogs out and returning the evening before Zameer was killed, which was a Saturday. Then she is seen taking the dogs out again on Sunday noon. In-between that, she appears to be holed up in her flat. She has a live-in maid called Nisha. We haven't questioned her as yet.'

Vikram is a bit disappointed, 'Hmm. A gap of just sixteen–seventeen hours in the camera recordings. It would have been physically impossible for her to make it to the island in time for the killing and back, in that time period.'

Tashi wonders, 'Maybe if she had a chartered plane and boat to take her there...'

Vikram seems unconvinced, 'Her building security tapes show her walking her dogs at 12.30 p.m. on Sunday. The possible killer was last sighted by the fishing trawler about 8.00 a.m. on Sunday. Not enough time to get back... Khurana, what happened to the satellite pictures?'

'They confirm the single boat travelling between the islands at the same time the beach boys and the fisherman saw it. Absolutely no other traffic other than the six fishing trawlers that we know about. Nothing around the reef island too.' Khurana replies.

'So they were right about the boat, wrong about Rumana? I don't get that. Any connection between Nicole and Rumana?'

Tashi is the one who answers, 'Rumana is a jet-setting party girl flitting from one exotic party location to another. Always chasing some hot celebrity. Nicole leads a quite disciplined life. She is a respected psychiatrist, an expert in trauma impact on the human brain.'

'Exactly,' says Khurana. 'She studies sick brains all day long and thrives on it. Won't be surprised if that made her crack up.'

'Or maybe she cures people who have no hope and gives them a reason to go on.' Tashi theorizes.

It's evident to Tashi that such thought processes are not a part of Khurana's mental makeup at all. Vikram is not only listening to the two of them; he is also watching them, watching their response to the murder suspect they are shadowing.

'So, as of now, both our suspects have strong alibis...' says Vikram.

'But it is Nicole's face!' says Khurana

Tashi, '...or a face like hers... Shekhar rebuilt from partials. There could be a twenty to thirty per cent margin of difference. Plus, the facial recognition software could have made allowances. She may not...'

Vikram cuts in, 'I need to get into her house.'

17

Moustache

The next morning.

Khurana calls, 'She is in the office, only the maid is home.'

Vikram and Tashi head for Nicole's flat. Vikram is dressed in loose faded pants and a shirt that's one size bigger. He has a moustache on.

'You should rethink that moustache...it's really too much,' says Tashi.

'Good, when I am gone she will remember only my bald head and the moustache' Vikram replies.

Mounted on the wall next to the door is a large painting of the Tree of Life. Strangely, it has been fixed upside down. Yet, it still makes sense. Vikram rings the bell, Tashi is on the lower landing, out of sight.

Nisha opens the door. Vikram flashes a photo ID: 'Narne Waterproofing.'

'We have been appointed by the apartment's committee office, I have to check the balcony and bathroom; water leakage downstairs,' he tells her.

Without waiting to be called in, he heads straight for the balcony and starts peering at the floor and walls. She follows him and watches him as he knocks and scrapes in places. He passingly notices several potted plants and gardening material.

Tashi peeps in through the open door, 'Does Joel Ghosh live here?'

Distracted, Nisha heads back to the door to talk to Tashi. Vikram takes the opportunity and rapidly enters the bedroom… then rapidly exits it. The two pugs come charging. One snaps at his heels, the other starts humping his ankle.

Tashi can see him through the doorway, comically skipping and kicking; trying to dislodge the dogs. Nisha hears the racket and races back.

'Hey… leave him… stop it… Sasha… Suzy…'

The dogs give her a bit of a run-around. She finally manages to grab them and rescue Vikram. Nisha is a little breathless, 'Sorry, they are a handful.'

Vikram makes a hasty retreat just as Sasha squirms out of Nisha's grip. In a flash, he is out of the house with the door firmly shut behind him.

As they leave the apartment, Tashi trails behind, not wanting him to see the irrepressible smirk on her face. So much for the super cool detective.

Back in the office, Vikram connects the concealed camera he had been wearing on his shirt, to the laptop. He watches the visuals several times, the hall, the balcony, the fleeting glimpse of the bedroom followed by the furry flurry of the dogs. Nothing stands out, nothing at all.

18

Is It?

Sunday morning. It's exactly a week since the killing. From the interior of an empty studio apartment overlooking Nicole's terrace, Vikram watches Nicole through a pair of powerful binoculars.

Dressed in yoga pants and a T, taking in the early morning sun, she looks stunning, but in a very different way. He takes a deep breath. It's the first time he is seeing her in person. There is no trace of the raw sexuality or violence of the woman atop Zameer. Her features are identical to the face now burnt in Vikram's mind, yet it is a far cry from the mesmeric image in Zameer's eyes.

He studies her face, her neck, shoulders, wrists, fingers. It's the acute focus of a lover admiring the object of his passion, or a predator stalking his prey. He is looking for the elusive body language that will prove to him that she could be the same woman in the video.

Nicole starts working on the carefully tended plants. The only violence she displays is in the nipping of the stem buds and bending of the wire to fix her bonsai. Even then, she seems to stop and talk to them.

She merely smiles when Nisha spills some tea as she hands over a steaming mugful. Suzie stretches benign at her feet, occasionally rolling over and prompting Nicole to scratch her belly. Sasha sticks his head out of the balcony railing to get a better look at the road below, then with some canine extrasensory perception, starts staring straight in Vikram's direction.

The picture of tranquillity jars Vikram.

Silence, until Khurana states the obvious, 'She somehow doesn't look it.'

Vikram eyes Khurana. His irritation about Raghav has been settling like a cloak around Khurana, Raghav's mole. Khurana, of course, is too thick-skinned to notice it.

'Maybe you can get a closer understanding of her...' says Vikram.

Late evening.

Nicole is jogging with her little pugs. She passes through a wooded grove. The pugs suddenly yank her in one direction. They can smell something interesting in the bush just beyond, she goes along and is soon screened from the main path by a hedge.

The dogs dive in and pull out a large bone. At the same instant, a hooded man grabs her and starts dragging her further into the bushes. The man is Khurana in disguise. It's an attack set up to provoke a response from her.

The whole grove is rigged with cameras, not unlike the beach where Zameer had been filmed.

Some distance away, Vikram and Tashi are watching the live feed on a laptop, searching for the telltale sign of aggression, posture—something that will match the woman they are searching for.

Khurana has grabbed her and is now overpowering her. Vikram and Tashi are tense, this is the moment she should turn... she doesn't...

Instead, she is begging, whimpering, squirming...there is nothing Khurana can do except shake her up since he is not supposed to really 'molest' her. Still, no fight, no strength, no aggression.

Somewhere in the fake grappling, Khurana loses control, one can't be too sure whether it's all a brilliant performance or a sliver of his inner animal surfacing. The pugs are creating a racket, snapping at Khurana's heels.

Nicole is choking, begging and struggling pitifully.

Tashi is distinctly disturbed, 'Stop...'

Vikram has already reached over and pressed a button. A speaker concealed in the bushes plays out the sound of footsteps approaching. It is Khurana's cue. He responds, just a fraction slower than he should have. Tashi and Vikram both register it. Then he drops Nicole and recedes into the bushes.

The dishevelled Nicole staggers to her feet. Panic-stricken and breathless, choking on sobs, she stumbles back to the main path and hurries off, constantly looking over her shoulder in panic. The pugs follow.

Khurana catches up with Vikram. He triumphantly displays a few strands of her hair that he had pulled out. Tashi has a distinct look of distaste as Khurana holds them up like a trophy.

The hair is dispatched for DNA testing. Vikram doesn't look hopeful.

19

New Normal

Next morning.

Vikram is in his office.

Voices raised in argument filter into the room. Before he can react, the door opens and Tashi enters, half dragging an angry, tearful Nicole. Khurana, looking extremely rattled, comes in behind them and quickly closes the door.

Tashi explains in an undertone, 'She came in to register a complaint about yesterday, with this sketch.'

She holds out an unflattering sketch of Khurana as he looked the night before, 'The local police station recognized Khurana, knew about her surveillance, so they called me.'

'This jerk is a policeman? And he tried to rape me! I will teach you a lesson you will never forget...' Nicole is fuming.

'Dr Nicole Augusto...' Vikram's cold voice cuts through and sharply silences her. 'You are the prime suspect in a murder case. We had the option of bringing you in and holding you in the lockup...or doing a "field test".'

This is completely unexpected and Nicole is shocked, 'Prime suspect? What killing? Field test? Molesting me was a field test, is...'

'Follow me,' Vikram tells her.

Tashi and Khurana are a little taken aback as they realize he is going to completely level with her. Vikram plays the film clip. The sexuality, the violence, has a sobering effect on Nicole. Then he shows her the image of her face, she gasps. He lets loose a barrage of questions to break her.

'Where were you on the fourteenth of this month? That is clear evidence putting you on the crime scene. What was the motive? Did he have a secret affair with you, made you his slave and then ditched you?' Then rapidly concludes, 'You are being arrested as a suspect for the killing of Zameer Khan.'

'No... No...I don't know... Never met...it's not me... not me...wait...' shocked and speechless, Nicole is unable to put up a coherent defence. Tashi and Khurana lose no time in formally arresting her, they rapidly take her fingerprint, take her pictures, and her handbag is submitted and noted.

Clang! She is put in a lock-up with two other women and the door has been shut. Khurana is especially relieved.

Tashi rapidly pulls the arrest record out of the general register. Zameer's murder is still a secret. This drama was just to shut Nicole up for the time being. Vikram, as usual, is breaking the law more than following it.

'So don't you want to report this to Raghav?' Tashi asks Khurana.

'Are you nuts? That stunt in the park is enough to get me grounded.'

Tashi can't conceal the smirk.

Khurana is suddenly enlightened, 'Shit! He could have easily played the attacker himself... But he made me do it so that...' Tashi laughs, 'He could grab your balls and squeeze them. Don't flatter yourself. He wanted to check out Nicole, getting you tangled up to stop you from reporting to Raghav, that was the bonus.'

'The bastard.'

Tashi shrugs, 'This is an investigation that doesn't even exist, there is no evidence, just shaky leads. Vikram has a track record of using all means, no matter how inappropriate…to get results.'

Khurana mulls on it. He is not going to let Vikram pull another stunt on him. 'What exactly was the reason for the disciplinary action against him?' he asks.

Tashi laughs, 'Several reasons. The last one was related to the rape and murder of Dr Rashmi Bhatia. The case against Sunny Mansingh, whom Vikram arrested, was dropped. Inconclusive circumstantial evidence. The crime was never solved. Three years later, Sunny was killed. In Vikram's home, with Vikram's service revolver. Vikram claimed he had shot him in self-defence. Sunny had been intimidating him for trying to reopen the case. The evidence was textbook perfect. Vikram walked free.'

'But no one believed it?'

'Rumour had it, Vikram set it up for Dr Bhatia's seventeen-year-old son and took the rap. The kid was never questioned. Returned shortly to Germany where he was studying.'

Khurana is speechless. Altruistic vigilante. That's not what he had expected of Vikram.

Tashi divulges more, 'There was a very strong rumour… Vikram was to collect a hefty sum from the Bhatia family for the killing…'

Khurana brightens up, this was more like it. 'So, he did it for the money.'

Tashi shrugs, 'Could be…though it doesn't really add up…'

'What's not to add up? It's perfect…'

'He would have made much more from Sunny's father to drop the case. Sunny should have had a mile-long record. His father, a three-time Member of Parliament was constantly bailing his son out. When Vikram walked free, the father wreaked mayhem on several people's career, including Raghav's: he lost out on several promotions. They got Vikram on some trivial procedural technicality in an unrelated case. He has been muzzled ever since and is seething.'

'Then Raghav is getting back at him by giving him this case?'

'Could be. Raghav knew this was a sticky one. But then, Vikram does have a sense, he does see things where others don't. Raghav is betting that if Vikram solves it, Raghav will take the credit. If Vikram fails, he can pull out Vikram's track record and have him suspended.'

'So, Vikram is a crazy bitter guy straining on the leash! And he doesn't like me. And Raghav is a vengeful top cop who wants to use me. Life is perfect.'

Tashi laughs, 'Relax, a few years in this twisted world and it'll seem normal.'

20

Habit... Repeat

Daybreak over Tokyo city. The lights on the Tower had been switched off. It stood like a grey streak against the dull grey rose skies.

Officer Katsuru enters his apartment after his night shift. He drops his gun and the Tokyo City Police badge on the table. Taller than an average Japanese, Katsuru has the face of a scholar, the ravages of a policeman's life had somehow not marked it.

Every Monday and Thursday, he spends one hour at the rapid dating café. Wednesday is to catch up with his sleep. Saturday is for an hour with one of his regular hookers. Unlike many Japanese men, fragile-looking teenaged girls held no fascination for him. He has always preferred his women older and stronger. Sundays are for his weekly visit to his five-year-old son, living with his ex-wife in Narita.

He is a man of habit and moderation, that's the way he sees himself.

Today is Tuesday, game–date day.

He boots on an elaborate gaming console, it's the highlight of his apartment. Vikram's voice filters into his earphones. 'Hey, Katsuru! Ready for another drubbing from the champ?'

Katsuru is rummaging through a closet filled with weird mutations of comic-con type costumes, 'I am fourteen thousand to your twenty thousand. That's nothing. I am going to kill you. Absolutely whack smash kill you.'

Vikram laughs. They are already online for the game.

Katsuru asks, 'Your avatar?'

Vikram is putting together his avatar for the game session. It's a lethal-looking woman warrior, with an uncanny resemblance to the killer he has been chasing.

Katsuru laughs, 'Ah! you can never get the cop out of the cop. So you are chasing a lady killer! Sexy babe. Lucky bastard.'

'Don't get smart with me. By those standards, your latest obsession is a mutant pig with a Mohawk haircut and tits!' That's exactly what Katsuru has assembled to be his online warrior. And that's very close to what he looks like, dressed in his cosplay costume. He takes a quick selfie and sends it to Vikram. Vikram yells back at him, 'You fucking sick pervert! That makes me feel dirty, thousands of miles away.'

Katsuru is pleased with the response and guffaws loudly. He removes the cover of a largish blobby shape to reveal an eerie luminescent sofa filled with some green gel. Then settles into it, munching a bag of dried shrimp snack.

Their easy friendship dates back many decades. They met as young boys when Vikram's father was posted as an attaché to the Indian Embassy in Japan. Katsuru's father, an official of parallel ranking in the Japanese government, invited the family over for dinner one summer evening.

The boys met and hit it off instantly. It was a friendship that had endured kinky 'boy games' and long disappearance on both sides. Katsuru had live-streamed his many attempts at losing his virginity—watched in the throes of explosive laughter by Vikram from halfway across the world. Both had been 'deflowered' by a drunken unknown fifty-year-old Japanese woman after much saki drinking amidst the cherry blossoms. They had sworn each other to a lifelong silence about the 'sordid' affair and stayed away from all further cherry blossom festivals.

That both had ended up choosing to be cops was a mere chance.

As the game progresses, it's clear that in a convoluted way, Vikram is trying to enact the aggression and violence to understand the killer. Vikram wins the first round. He lets out a string of celebratory curses. Bang! Bang! There is loud rapid banging on his locked bedroom door, it finally penetrates through his headphones.

He opens the door to find Anand standing there waving his mobile phone in his face.

'Some Tashi…you've missed like…ten calls…What are you…?'

Vikram grabs the phone and reads the latest text, races out without any explanation.

On the headphone, Katsuru's voice is still spilling through. Vikram's avatar gets shot point-blank by Katsuru. It's Katsuru's turn to cheer and taunt Vikram. He gets no response. Vikram hasn't bothered to log out or tell him that he is leaving.

Katsuru gets a request for a duel from another online gamer with a Billie Eilish clone avatar. He moves on.

The interior of a screening room.

Raghav, Vikram, Tashi and Khurana watch another snuff killing video unfold.

This time, it's a rising cricket star, Suraj Singh. It's at night, on a boat, surrounded by darkness except for some far off fireworks on the shore. But it's the same method, the same sex and death routine.

Raghav frowns, 'She's turned into a serial killer.'

'My guess…she's been one for a while. That lady has a real heavy-duty past hidden someplace,' declares Vikram.

Silence.

His conclusion is indisputable. Instantly, the weight of their responsibility has multiplied many times over.

Raghav finds himself glaring at Vikram with completely misplaced anger. Why is it that anything Vikram touches goes nuts? This case just spiralled into a dark hole.

As Vikram, Tashi and Khurana leave, Vikram returns Raghav's glare, 'Guess this film was also passed on to you by some sicko from your club crimson.'

Out in the corridor. Tashi is smirking, 'Club crimson! Where the hell did you get that from?'

Vikram laughs, 'From you. That's the shade of lipstick you carry in your purse but never wear.'

Tashi stops in her tracks, speechless for once.

Unrepentant Vikram continues, 'What are you waiting for, the right man to turn up?'

Khurana mutters to her, 'I can't believe it, you are letting him get away with that.'

Vikram laughs, 'What can she say? She has been nosing around my office, my desk, my washroom…searching for what, Tashi?'

Tashi walks off, silent.

21

Timeline

On a whiteboard, Vikram creates a timeline of Suraj's movements before his death.

> Sunday evening, 6 p.m., Suraj Singh left his team's net practice.
> 6.15 p.m., appearance at a celebrity party.
> 6.30 p.m., left party. Not seen again.
> 8.15–8.30 p.m. Fireworks display at Shells Resort for a wedding party, the only one-of-its-kind in the area. Hence, possibly the one visible in the film.
> So, possible time of death, 8.15–8.30 p.m., Sunday.

Tashi points out, 'Today is Tuesday. The upload has been much later than the last time.'

'It's not Nicole. On Sunday, we were in the park with her when the killing happened and since Monday, she has been in the lock-up,' says Khurana.

'…not Rumana either, her remand ends tomorrow.' Tashi adds.

Silence. Both primary suspects have been knocked off in one stroke.

Vikram calls Shekhar, the techie, 'Am sending you a film.'

'Make my day! You have some collection.'

'I want an immediate report, search frame by frame for a face…'

22

Insider

Khurana enters Vikram's office. He looks disturbed, 'Nicole's lawyer is here, wants to know the charges.'

Tashi interrupts on a video call. She is in the hotel tracking Suraj Singh's movements.

'Guess who I found in the hotel surveillance tapes…' She turns her mobile to a frozen frame on the surveillance screen in the security room of the hotel, it's unmistakably Rumana.

Vikram is stunned, 'What the fuck!'

'She was released sometime Friday evening. Her father, Rakesh Dhawan, was giving Raghav's office a hard time it seems…'

In a fit of rage, Vikram calls Raghav, 'Why the fuck did you release Rumana?' Raghav is about to explode but stops when he hears the next line. 'She has been in the same hotel as Suraj Singh since she left the lock-up. If I prove she is the killer then Suraj's death is on your mother-fucking head.'

Bang! Vikram hangs up.

Khurana squirms.

Vikram orders, 'Release Nicole from custody.'

Khurana is very nervous. But trying to argue with Vikram when he is in such a dark mood is not going to get him anywhere. He braces himself for what is to come and goes to do as told.

Nicole is released. Vikram watches as she has a brief chat with her lawyer. The lawyer seems to be shaking his head, advising against something. She seems to be adamant. The lawyer shrugs and leaves. She heads for Vikram's office, catches him looking at her. Their eyes lock, she heads straight for him. The hours in the lock-up seem to have taken a toll on her body but not her spirit.

'I will not register an attempted rape complaint against you guys...on one condition. From this minute onwards, you will share every detail of the case with me,' she tells him.

A prime suspect holding them at ransom, demanding to be made an insider. This lady is turning out to be interesting. Vikram is certainly surprised but conceals it well.

Nicole adds, 'Someone out there is impersonating me, using my face. I want to know who, why. I want it stopped...for you it's a job, for me it's personal.'

A specialization in post-trauma criminal psychology, with over a thousand case studies. Vikram mulls, then seems to come to a conclusion. 'Our killer is certainly a fucked up character... having you onboard would be an advantage. Welcome to the team, Dr Nicole.'

It's time for Nicole to be surprised, she had come mentally prepared to face stiff resistance.

'Ok... Good...good...'

Vikram declares, 'I'm not doing this because of your threat. I am doing it because I think you can actually help. There was another killing. We know that was not done by you. Khurana, complete the formality that permits us to take her in as a domain expert.'

Khurana, taken aback by the turn of events, is nonetheless relieved that his ass is once again safe. He hustles her out.

Tashi walks in, 'You've got to be joking! True, it wasn't her with Suraj Singh, but what about Zameer's killing?'

'I thought, in the park, you were convinced it was not her.'

'Yes, but what I feel is immaterial... It totally looks like her face in the film! That could very well be her in the act! And the DNA result matching her hair with the hair on the beach hasn't come in as yet. We can't write her off to the point that we make her an insider!'

Vikram shrugs, 'If she's the killer, let's hope she makes that one little mistake that helps us put her away. If she is not the killer then we need to tap her brains...find the killer. Why is her face in the film? Why?'

Tashi doesn't have an answer but doesn't seem convinced by Vikram's reasoning either. Her feminine instinct is picking up something else.

'You've the hots for her!' she accuses.

'What? Are you nuts?'

Tashi walks away unconvinced. Vikram snorts. Women!... then starts tracking Rumana in the hotel security tapes that Tashi has just brought in.

Rumana checks into the hotel. She doesn't look any worse from her stint in the lock-up. She seems to be raring to get some action. Did she really spend any time in the lock-up or had Roddy been bullied into setting her free much earlier than the order from Raghav's office? With a father as influential as hers, anything was possible.

On the day of the killing, she steps out of the elevator at 6 p.m. Wearing a chic 'Ashes of Roses' short dress teamed with a striking bead necklace, she walks into the party. Within moments of entering the room, she is hugging and air-kissing people around her.

6.15 p.m. She is barely a few feet away from Suraj Singh as he enters. He goes through the routine of greeting and backslapping people. She seems unaware of his presence. A few minutes later, as she heads to the other end of the room she almost brushes past him. She looks at him, but he is distracted, doesn't notice her.

Vikram watches the clip over and over again, searching for anything of significance. Nothing at all. There was never any eye contact between the two.

6.45 p.m. Suraj starts making his way to the exit. Rumana is visible, heading for the bar. The screen splits into two. Parallel footage from the party, the elevator and the hotel exterior surveillance camera. Suraj, as he steps out of the hotel, has his hoodie up and walks off into the street, out of camera range. It's a clear warm night, there is no reason for the hoodie to be covering his head. But Suraj Singh needed it, stars like him don't exactly saunter down the road and head out for a hot date. He had to cover his identity. He was heading someplace that he wanted to keep super-secret.

7.30 p.m. Rumana is at the bar, giggling with a man.

8.00 p.m. In the lift, on the way to her room with the man. As she steps out into the corridor, she is swinging her necklace above her head, making strange rotor blade noises. She is obviously high on something.

Vikram asks, 'What is the possibility of Suraj heading off with a woman he had just met?'

'Quite possible. He had a reputation of being...not picky.' Tashi replies.

'Hmm. But the killer has to be picky. The timing, the boat, the cameras... Everything.'

'The date had to be preplanned.'

'Maybe it was not the first time either.'

Tashi is set to leave, 'We need to look into all his communication. They planned the date, there has to be something somewhere.'

'Rumana?' Vikram wants to know.

'Still holed up with the man in her room. Should we bring her in?' Tashi asks.

Vikram shrugs off the suggestion, 'For what? Appearing on surveillance tapes with a perfect alibi each time a man is killed? Have her watched.'

23

Non Sync

The small lobby outside Vikram's office has been converted into a makeshift data centre. The glass door is firmly shut. The sudden activity in the otherwise sleepy office has created a buzz on the entire floor. Theories are floating.

Tashi is behind a desk, inundated with the data flowing in about Suraj's phone calls, pictures and videos from his laptop, notes left for him at the hotel, fan mail, fan blogs, news articles, piles of gifts and cards left for him in the rooms.

Shekhar has loaned her one of his geeks to run through Suraj's laptop. Pale, skeletal thin with large saucer-like eyes, he is thirty but looks barely eighteen. The geek doesn't seem to blink at all. Tashi counts herself blinking four times to his nil. It's the long hours staring at the screen, she decides. Soon, humanity will evolve to having no eyelids at all. She is filled with a sense of pity for him.

The geek, in turn, is uncomfortable in the company of this physically alpha female. She is the type he would pay to sex-cam, but in real life, he wouldn't willingly have anything to do with her. He immediately puts on a pair of large red headphones and starts listening to deep-sea whale sounds.

The geek's name is Lakshya Chattopadhyay, everyone called him Laks, till someone discovered his secret online ID is @ithekong. Inspired by King Kong. It was so utterly ludicrous, the usual crazy logic happened and now he is called @kong.

The high point of @kong's life happened eight years ago.

In Paris. Wearing a Guy Fawkes mask, he had walked with the Anonymous for a whole block before losing his nerve and slinking back to his college dorm. It was an adrenaline rush he treasured.

To Vikram, perched on Tashi's table, he might as well be invisible.

Vikram calls Khurana, 'Scan all the footage from the hotel security cameras during his entire stay in the hotel...and all earlier stays there during the past one year.'

'Sure. The traffic signal's security camera immediately outside the hotel was working. He walked past it three minutes after leaving the hotel. Alone.'

'...and then?'

'Nothing, he did not reach the next junction on either side.'

'Any private cameras? There are two jewellery shops and a McDonalds down the right...'

'He didn't show up on any of them. Must have taken the left. That goes through a basti, so no cams at all.'

'So, basically, we lost him the moment he stepped out of the hotel.'

In walks Vikram's friend, Dr Anand.

Vikram looks at him, 'What the fuck took you so long?'

'I was squeezing out the pus from the bum boil of a debauched seventy-year-old granny with a...'

He pauses when he catches sight of Tashi, who is looking at him coldly.

Vikram makes the introduction, 'This is Dr Anand. This is Tashi.' Anand returns Tashi's cold stare then deciding that she passes some strident test in his head, he offers her a smashed up packet of chewing gum. Tashi takes one look at his grubby palm and refuses.

Vikram heads to the screening room, 'Come in, you two.'

He starts Suraj's video.

'He is probably high on some drug, look how the pupil doesn't respond even when bright light falls on it. Need a blood sample to identify the drug though,' says Anand.

He mimics Suraj's grinding motion in the sexual act. Tashi watches him, repulsed and amused. Then she realizes that the man is in dead earnest.

'Notice the subtle jerkiness in his movements,' Anand points out.

On the screen, Suraj is on top of the woman. When played back in slow motion, the visuals do reveal the slight jerky spasms in what should have been a smooth flowing riding motion. Vikram switches to normal speed, 'Unlike Zameer's film that was totally silent, she has allowed the audio to remain in some parts.'

Suraj Singh is repeating violent sexual expletives in his native Haryanvi, in a guttural tone. He seems to be in some kind of a loop as he says them over and over again. Anand is chanting the same expletives in the same rhythm, he and Suraj are out of sync.

'...heavy tongue... That means there is a response delay, it's some kind of neurological inhibitor,' Anand takes a guess.

'That's not affecting his...performance though,' Vikram mutters.

'The substance is slowing him, his natural fitness is pushing its way through. Shit! You guys get to jerk off on this while I get to examine snorty teenagers and ancient aunties with gas problems, life sucks!'

Out of spite, Vikram fast forwards the video to the killing and Anand sees the gory end. He winces, 'Shit, it's going to be a long time before I let a woman on top of me.'

Tashi is amused, he doesn't exactly look like a guy that women are fighting to get on top of.

An hour later.

Anand is gone. Vikram, Tashi and Khurana are mulling over things. Finally, Vikram says, 'She has made critical changes in the filming. The focus is on Suraj, she has taken pains to ensure that even the immediate background is not visible. Had it not been for the unexpected fireworks…this could have been anywhere in the world.'

'If Anand's analysis is right, she drugged Suraj before the act, we don't know if she did that with Zameer too. Suraj wouldn't have voluntarily taken any drug whilst he was in the midst of international matches,' says Tashi.

'With Zameer, she may not have needed to drug him, Zameer's fit look was meant only for his films. Suraj was at another level altogether. A young man at the top of his game, he was superfit. Maybe she was levelling the field a bit, by drugging him,' wonders Vikram.

Khurana is trying to zero down on the coordinates of where the boat could have been when Suraj was killed. He triangulates on a five by five square kilometres off the western shore of India. He looks at Vikram, 'Could have been any of these twenty to thirty boats. Without an identifying mark of the boat…can't say.'

The killer had taken great care to leave no identifying features visible, and the darkness had done the rest.

Shekhar calls in, 'The audio track has only one voice. Suraj's. Nothing else. In all likelihood, an ultra near field microphone was placed next to his head. The sounds he made overwhelmed everything else, even her breathing.'

Vikram is impressed, 'The precise spot where he would die was marked, and she managed to get him there…'

'We circulated Rumana's picture, some recognized her but nobody connected her with Suraj last evening.' Tashi says.

Khurana adds, 'Last week, a model was signed to shoot a health drink ad-film with Suraj. She showed up with bruises that makeup couldn't cover. She lost the assignment. Blamed him, she had spent the night with him. He was amused, claimed that she had enjoyed it. If a woman wants to be stud-fucked she can't complain about it getting rough.'

'He said that?' Tashi wants to know.

'Yes...kind of, I mean... I am saying...that's how it would be, right?'

Tashi is staring at Khurana with undisguised disgust, this man's creep quotient is endless. Vikram is amused by her and laughs out loud. Tashi lashes out, 'You guys are sick, maybe our killer's got it right.'

Evening. Jogging track. Raghav is jogging, his two bodyguards trailing several metres behind. Vikram joins him.

Raghav says to him, 'Unlike Bollywood, playing truant in the cricket world is unacceptable. It doesn't make you a bigger star, it gets you out of the team. Suraj Singh's absence in today's friendly match has been noticed and there are a dozen theories floating. Anytime now, it will hit "breaking news". Rumana's alibi?'

'Surveillance tapes again!'

Raghav breathes a bit easy, but realizes that twice in the proximity of the victim...can't be a coincidence. Or can it be? Vikram continues, 'You release suspects without informing me, don't give me access to the source of the videos. You tie my hands and expect me to perform!'

'Look. The source is too big and important to be compromised for just homicide.'

'Just homicide? You are kidding me! These aren't some freaking drunks getting run over. These are two of the most famous men in the country!'

Raghav merely shrugs, 'Our country does not have the expertise to scan the worldwide net, but there are…others who do. They pass on stuff to us, we reciprocate in different ways. They simply watch, collect data and report, they do not investigate; that would reveal their presence and that is unacceptable.'

Vikram is annoyed, 'Don't give me that stuff. I need access to the website, to payment gateways. The money collected to see the films, that's the trail back to the killer.' Raghav is adamant, 'You will have to find another way.'

Vikram stops jogging. Raghav realizes he is talking to himself. Vikram is gone.

Vikram needs to clear his head. Disconnect. No better way to achieve that than hang out with complete strangers. He heads to the pub, orders a drink, cracks a joke with the bartender. The man next to him hears and chuckles. Before long, a few more men have joined in the impromptu exchange of jokes.

The challenge of keeping strangers entertained with his wit makes him relax.

In the background, the TV is on, muted. One of the guys looks up and notices something. It's a face; Vikram's face. There is a news item on the disappearance of the cricketer Suraj Singh.

Vikram's radar has picked up the change in the man's body language as he tries to link the image on the screen with Vikram. He catches sight of the reflection of the TV on a shiny surface. It's a bad picture, but it's him alright. It's the news of Suraj Singh's disappearance breaking out and somehow he and the team have been named as the investigators.

Even as the man is about to connect it and say something,

Vikram slips away. By the time the gang looks up at the TV, the anchor has moved on to the next story.

'It was him, I swear…just wait, the news will come back,' the man in the bar is saying to people around him.

Vikram curses under his breath as he gets into his car. How the hell did his involvement get out? His mobile phone vibrates. He pulls it out. It's a WhatsApp message from an unknown number, with a video link. He stares at it for a long time.

24

I

Interior of the screening room. Vikram, Tashi, Khurana and Nicole. Vikram plays the video clip he received. They watch.

The film opens to reveal a darkened room, they can see the outline of a seated woman. Details of her face and body contours are lost to the deep shadows of the room. She speaks in a monotone whisper. The boundaries of the room are not visible. She could be in a small cell or a large warehouse...

'I am obsessed with the need to talk, to tell you my story. Will you listen to me? Please, without passing judgment?' the woman begins.

A rapid kitschy montage starts, it is created from dozens of YouTube videos to match the story she narrates.

The woman's whispering voice continues over the videos, 'My mother was a whore in Casablanca. Five hundred bucks a trick. The Blue Moor Club was where she worked, sailors from the dock would swing open the doors on their brass hinges, their eyes wild with lust from weeks on the water.

I remember her. So pretty she was, so full of life. Home was just above the bar, mommy's bed was right next to mine, only she'd never sleep in it at night.

"Never get into the guilt trip." She would tell me each time we walked home from church. I was just a little girl, barely ten.

"Face it, your mom is a whore. We will never know who your father is. Now, when you grow up, you can be anyone you want—a doctor, a cop, a nun, a business tycoon—why not? I got no problem with that. You want to be a whore, I got no problem with that as well—only do it better than I did. Get your act together, think big. Go to college. Get a real degree. Start your own swanky whorehouse—squeeze the johnnies real hard; they love it only when it hurts."

Mom was like that. Unrepentant and truthful—right until the day she died.'

Visuals of a burial. The freshly filled grave with the little girl sitting next to it, not wanting to go home.

Nighttime, visuals put together of a brutal rape. Three men take turns. The victim is never visible but it is obvious that it's the little girl.

The second man has a broken gold tooth, the right incisor, it is magnified more and more as he towers over her…till it pixelates, becomes unrecognizable and fills the whole screen. The impression created is that the little girl fixated on it, blocked everything off.

The woman in the dark is once again visible on the screen, she is still.

'I searched for that tooth for a long time…never found it.'

The film becomes another montage. Next morning finds the little girl sprawled on her mother's grave. The morning drizzle has drenched her, the bloodstains on her dress are hardly visible amongst the mud stains. Teardrops and raindrops are indistinguishable. She is willing herself to die, get absorbed into the same earth under which her mother lies.

Her voice carries on, 'I prayed for the earth to swallow me, take me to my mother lying beneath.'

The gravedigger finds her there. Strong arms lift her gently from the mound, she is too frozen in shock, pain and cold to notice. The same priest who buried her mother carries her away.

'But I am my mother's daughter and I found my strength… never again would any man do this to me.'

As the montage comes to an end, so does the monologue. The woman from the shadows steps out. Everyone is stunned. Most of all Nicole, as she sees herself on screen.

The woman—Nicole—on the screen continues, 'I always admired you, wanted to be you, this face is my tribute to you.'

The film clip ends.

Three hard faces are staring at Nicole: Vikram, Khurana and Tashi.

Nicole is clearly shaken, 'What? She just admitted she wants to be me…that's not me!'

'Who is it?' Vikram asks.

'I…I don't know.'

'You have to know her.'

'I have treated so many women. Her story, of the loss and abuse, it's the story of so many women out there. She could be any of them.'

'No…not every woman has the ability to turn into that. Think.'

Tashi asks, 'Why did she send it? Why reveal this about herself?'

Vikram snaps back, 'She didn't reveal a damn thing. She never mentioned the killings, just told us a sob story, which may be her story or some random bullshit. There is no way we can link this to the killings and claim she is the killer.'

Tashi persists, 'But she had Nicole's face.'

Nicole has recovered a bit, 'It's a clever game. She is teasing.'

Vikram mulls, 'She sent this, directly to me. She knew about the investigation, she knows about us.'

'By now the whole country knows about us,' says Khurana.

Vikram's mind has raced ahead, 'About us, yes. But the fact that Nicole is with us, no. She sent it to me yet spoke to Nicole at the end of it. She knew Nicole would see it. She is watching us.'

His conclusion is beyond doubt. Everyone mulls on that. She has changed the rules of the investigation irrevocably.

'Some of the details that came out effortlessly…like the five hundred bucks for a trick, brass hinges of the swinging doors of the club her mother worked from, the broken right gold incisor of her rapist—such extreme detail comes only when you are narrating an experience,' says Nicole.

'She did this to connect herself with you Nicole. She knows you… You know her. Her identity is hidden in your memory, in your records. Find it.' Vikram urges her.

'Maybe she is leading us to discover her? Recognition is important for a killer' ego…' Khurana says.

'…or she wants to point us in the wrong direction and throw us off the scent completely…' Tashi tries to bring in a fresh theory.

Vikram interrupts, 'Stop. We do not know her mind, we will not assume to know her logics. For now, just flow with the evidence. She knows Nicole, so Nicole knows her. Nicole, you have to find her, that's all.'

Tashi is surprised at this new-found caution in Vikram. This was a man whose twisted logic, justified planting drugs on one suspect and sexually molesting another. Was this middle age kicking in? No. He was seeing something, she wasn't.

@kong finds himself with a new task. The video has been given to him. Now, he has to trace its source. Within minutes, he knows the URL is useless, the number from which the WhatsApp message was received is also useless. It is a camouflage, no point looking in that direction. Feeling suitably challenged, he starts looking at the visuals in the film. Trying to identify the original videos from which the kitschy montages were edited. It's going to be a long night, but he is hooked.

He retires out of sight into the back office at the end of the corridor, wanting to be left alone to enjoy the digital chase he is embarking on.

Nicole and Khurana leave, they head back to her clinic.

Tashi and Vikram are silent, pensive. 'I don't get it... Why did she send it?' Tashi breaks the silence.

'Because, she has gotten away with the kills, that's why. She wants to gloat, to tease, to plain drive us crazy...to keep us running in circles.'

'But then, by following her lead and looking into Nicole's records, we would be doing just that.'

'Yes. She must see us running in circles...then again, it may throw up something...'

He returns to studying the clip again. The moment she stepped out of the shadows and revealed Nicole's face. The tilt of the head, the hairline, the angle of the heeled toes as she took the half step forward. The body speaks as much as the words you choose.

An hour later Nicole and Khurana walk in carrying boxes full of Nicole's case studies and records. Tashi follows with a load of junk food. They are settling in for a long haul.

While Tashi and Nicole sort out the records for inspection, Khurana is dishing out the goodies, '....medium thin crust with tandoori chicken, mushrooms and double cheese... sandwich with extra olives and mustard...that's the green apple slush...'

Vikram looks on disapprovingly, 'Honestly guys, this is not a picnic!'

Then he grabs one box and disappears into his inner office

before anyone can react. Tashi's mobile phone beeps, she checks it and follows Vikram in.

'The DNA report just came. The hair on the beach does not match Nicole's. That clears her in both the killings,' she says.

Vikram nods, 'Our killer could be in one of those boxes.' He opens his pizza box, 'Will you take this, it has mushrooms, I hate mushrooms.'

Tashi holds out her sandwich, 'Veg with mustard.'

Vikram waves it off with disgust. Tashi returns to the outer office. He removes the mushroom from his pizza with tweezers kept for collecting evidence. Then munching on his pizza, he watches the three of them. They have moved into the open office verandah. The city lights twinkle behind them.

Nicole's animosity towards Khurana seems to have thawed.

The man who could be a standup comic with such ease has completely disappeared. The twinkle that he could so easily conjure in his eyes is also switched off. There is a dark brooding stillness about him. This is Vikram, himself, not wearing any face other than his own.

He watches Nicole closely, alternately staring at the digitally created image of her face on his phone. With a heightened awareness, he focuses sharply on her every gesture, her every movement. Inside his head, there is a jam of images trying to push their way up into his conscious mind.

The way she adjusts the hem of her dress, the manner in which she crosses her legs, the tiny flick of her tongue when she feels the drop of mayonnaise on her lips. The way she stops the cup of coffee from sliding down the armrest of her chair then makes a game of it. The unconscious sensuality in her movements, her fingers moving almost like a dance on the coffee cup.

He relives the memory of observing her for the first time, in her terrace. The slight raise in her eyebrow when she suppresses an expression, the blinking when she takes time to answer, the woman in the film revealing her face as Nicole's...

Back to the present.

Nicole catches him watching her through the glass partition. Her eyes hold no mystery when she smiles, he finds himself smiling back at her. He turns away. Unknown to her, he is still observing her through a series of cross-reflections and brooding.

His mobile phone beeps. He is wanted in the forensic lab.

25

Amazon

Interior of the forensic lab. Vikram walks in, joins the head lab technician Jaspal Singh. Short and circular is the only way to describe this devout Sikh. Jaspal looks more like a highway dhaba cook, in charge of the earthen oven, churning out tandoori chickens.

He is, in fact, one of the sharpest men in his field. Gifted with that extra sense that leads him to look for things by intuition. and the tenacity to follow through on his intuitions. Jaspal believes no evidence is also evidence.

'Your crime scene, where Zameer was killed, was cleaned by an expert. She used this…'

There is a miniature drone on his table, much like the hovering gadget that the killer had set up on the beach.

'What is that?'

'An incinerator mounted on a drone. It's used to clean up contaminated areas in labs dealing with highly contagious pathogen.'

'Right, but what did she do with it?'

'Let me show you.'

Jaspal operates it with a remote. It lifts off the ground. He lowers it into a glass tray with sand. On his command, four sharp jets of superheated air come out of the lower flap and drill into the sand. 'The intense heat is burning up all organic matter in the sand, she burnt up all your clues: skin cells, blood cells, miniature organisms that may have fed on these cells, hair… Look.'

Vikram watches bits of hair and human nail shrivel and turn to ash in the sand, 'I get the picture.'

Jaspal continues, 'She would have gotten away with it…had Tashi not taken the sand samples from different depths. This sample came from the top, this from two inches below the surface, this from three inches… They show a decreasing level of carbon content. The carbon is from the ashes of the burnt organic matter.'

'So in erasing the evidence, she left a clue of having erased the evidence…'

'Yes, Sir!'

'That was good sleuthing. This incinerator, it's a highly specialized gadget, how would one lay a hand on it?'

'I got this on Amazon.'

'What the fuck! This homicide-erasing freak is on Amazon? Then anyone could have laid their hands on it.'

Vikram is about to stride off when it occurs to him, she was so damn meticulous, yet he had found Zameer's skin cells and the unidentified hair, right out there in the open… How is that possible? He is tired, he heads home.

Late night. Back in the office.

Khurana is ready to call it a day. He suggests that they should all call it a day. Tashi ignores him. He leaves. Somewhere out of sight @kong continues his quest to crack the video Vikram gave him.

Tashi is studying a pile of patients' reports. A monotony has set in. Nicole was right. The same story of abuse, pain, confusion… over and over again. Nicole is at the other end of the corridor. She is scanning the confidential video and audio recordings taken during her sessions with patients. Tashi has shortlisted two possible suspects and their details are pinned up on her board.

Nicole drops in with two cups of green tea. Taking a new box, she returns to her cubicle.

Sometime later, Tashi catches sight of Nicole pacing the floor, reading a folder. Tashi stifles a yawn. She gets up, stretches her legs, and does a couple of pushups to fight off sleep, sits down on the sofa.

26

Cringe

Tashi wakes up from a deep sleep, Vikram is shaking her, repeating Khurana's name over and over.

A distraught Nicole, dishevelled from a night on the office sofa, is pacing about.

Tashi gets up with a start, 'What? What happened?'

Vikram's face is a mask set in granite. He marches off to the screening room. Tashi and Nicole rush after him.

Tashi enters the room to see an absurdly grinning and gyrating Khurana on the big screen. He is in a film. A chill sets into her bones.

It's late into the night. He is lit by the headlights of a car. He is near-naked and doing a cringe-worthy striptease. It's obvious he feels he is being real sexy and 'fun'.

With a deep sense of foreboding, Tashi sinks into a chair.

On the screen, a woman steps into the camera frame, with her back to the camera. In one stroke she rips off the slinky short dress she is wearing and turns it into a whip. She starts whipping Khurana's butt with it, he just whoops and wiggles some more.

Vikram notices that both Nicole and Tashi grimace at the sheer bad taste.

The woman starts circling him. Her body is visible at times, never her face. She is down to a bikini bottom and nipple guards. As she comes fully around, her face is visible to the camera for just a fleeting moment.

Tashi gets a jolt, it's her face. The killer is pretending to be Tashi!

Biting back her response, she continues watching intently. Vikram is watching both women closely.

In the film, Tashi and Khurana are on an isolated jetty. She continues to tease Khurana and make a complete clown of him. Then with a remote, she switches off the car's headlights and runs towards the water.

Khurana follows. It's a cloudless full moon night, they are clearly visible. He picks her off her feet, she lets him. Once more, the pattern of cameras filming them is the same. Two cameras set to a wide angle, clearly showing them full body. The killer is wearing one camera on her body with the precise intent of catching Khurana's expressions up-close.

The two of them tumble on to the ground, Khurana is now visible in close shots.

He has just been brought into position for the third and fourth cameras, set at the precise focus needed to get him up close.

The predictability of the act is sickening. On-screen, a sixth sense kicks in for Khurana, he begins to recognize a pattern. Next moment, he finds himself airborne and brought crashing down on his back, under her. Now, the panic on his face is clearly visible.

She moves faster this time, at lightning speed. There is no caressing of the torso, just rapid sharp blows. He does his best to heave his hips upwards to throw her off. She has a vice-like grip on him. He is no match for her strength or expertise. The ritual follows its pattern, the jugular yanked off once again, he is dead.

She punches towards the sky with the flesh and blood dripping down her hand, then throws back her head and enacts a silent animal howl. A victory celebration. Her silhouette framed against the full moon and silvery waves makes an incredibly stunning image.

27
Lurker

Bright sunny day. In an embassy enclave. Vikram and Raghav surrender their mobile phones and are politely guided to a corridor.

They move through it knowing fully well that as they walked, a dozen different scanners are searching their bodies for anomalies. Body contour, size, shape, thermal… Vikram is pretty sure they knew about the metal filling in his third left molar and the two-inch metal rod in his right arm.

He asks Raghav, 'How come your super-secret source wants to see me now? Why couldn't this have happened before? Poor Khurana might have remained alive.'

Raghav is sulky and silent. The death of Khurana is sitting heavy on him, but Vikram is in no mood to be sympathetic.

Sitting on the rolling lawns, with Raghav and Vikram, is a hawk-faced man of indeterminate nationality.

'I am Smith. We are sorry you lost your man.'

Vikram is unable to keep the sarcasm from his voice, 'Yes, so are we…Mr Smith.'

Raghav is glaring at him, *behave, they don't have to do this*, he seems to be indicating.

'You must appreciate that our priorities are global security, not kinky sex kills,' says Smith. 'We spread a wide net and invariably stuff gets caught in it. Occasionally, we do pass on information to the relevant authorities in the countries concerned.'

Vikram recognizes that he has entered a world with its own

rules and morality. Unapologetic and sharply focused at a bigger picture that stretches out into the future. Then why were they talking to him?

Smith holds out an iPad at Vikram, 'This website came up a few hours before Khurana's killing. Lasted four minutes. The connection was made only after Khurana's death video came along this morning, on a completely separate website.'

Vikram studies the kitschy website. Its styling is similar to the video sent to him by the killer, pretending to be Nicole. It has images of Tashi, Khurana and himself.

Tashi's image is a selfie. Vikram's is an unflattering mugshot, seems to be taken after a week-long drinking spree. Khurana is posing like a stud, showing his six-pack in a pair of really brief florescent swimming trunks. He looks every bit the cocksure arsehole he was.

Under each image is a running counter. The numbers reveal the bets placed on them. The betting stops, the unknown bidders have chosen Khurana. Five million euros! With a single image, he had managed to grate on the nerves of enough men and women across the world and had been chosen to die. The clock shows India time: 9.30 p.m.

Vikram lets out a low whistle, he is impressed. Raghav breathes heavily.

Vikram speaks, 'By 9.30 that evening, we were all on the breaking news as investigators of Suraj Singh's murder. First, she made us celebrities, then turned us into a game...and then she enchased it!'

'She was hunting her hunters, timed it so perfectly... Khurana would not have gone off with an unknown woman in the midst of a case like this...' Raghav seems puzzled.

Vikram looks at Raghav, 'Oh! I think your budding protégé

was fool enough...but then again she may have cultivated him, pretending to be Tashi and waited to strike at the right...most lucrative moment.'

Then looking at Smith, he asks, 'Was Zameer's the first video she made?'

'We don't know, it was the first we caught because there was a celebrity involved.'

'The finesse with which she is making them and the cover-up...seems like she had practice and help.'

Smith shrugs, 'You must understand where we found this. The visible Internet as the public knows—Gmail, Twitter, Facebook, Instagram, Wikipedia, Google search engines—it is only ten per cent of the Internet.'

'And you are the lurkers of the vast unknown?'

'Something like that...the vast ninety per cent of the Internet remains concealed in private servers and storages, phantom identities and networks across the world. It's popularly called the Dark Web, the shadow web. Those who operate here are obsessed with secrecy. Corporates, government agencies, activists, vigilantes, criminals, reporters, hackers and sometimes just plain bored teenagers killing time. A lot that happens here is absolutely legit...but it is also a place for concealing secrets, sharing secrets and forming communities that would not be accepted in some countries and in an open society.

'It's a place beyond any country's jurisdiction... No man's land, that's what we call it.

'The darkest side of humanity also comes alive here. Criminals, terrorists...it can get lawless and wild. Its users run into many thousands, they are like fleeting shadows, they keep appearing and disappearing, each time in different forms and identities. Encryption and proxies reign. Networks are designed to erase all trails. It's only when their cyber lives spill into real life and leave a trail of mayhem that they become visible…and that's where this came up.'

As Raghav grapples with the load that Smith has just dumped on them, he has a sinking feeling. He has heard it all before. But this is the first time he is having to deal with this first-hand. The world was moving faster than he could keep up with.

Vikram's mind has more pressing queries, 'So, does the Red Room exist?'

'What's the red room?' Raghav asks.

'A maybe not so mythical place that exists in the dark net where killings happen online for money.'

Smith adds, 'Usually, it's some unidentifiable tramp…or a refugee…and it happens in dark unidentifiable rooms by people wearing masks…who knows when, where…real…staged…'

'But why is it not pursued?' Vikram wants to know.

'As far as we are concerned, it's collateral damage. We cannot pursue it and reveal our presence to other more lethal players in this no man's land, on whom we have spent years, and millions tracking.'

'But this time it was different. Zameer was a well-known superstar, so it would come out sooner or later anyway. Right?' Vikram asks.

Smith nods, 'Also, the location was identifiable, so we passed it on to your government. Our only condition being that the killing is to be revealed after the killer is found and with a suitable back story in place. Under no circumstances is our connection to be revealed. We did not expect this rapid escalation of kills.'

Vikram is not done, 'The money collected for Zameer's and Suraj's killings?'

Smith shakes his head, 'We don't have that. Must have been

a non-linked website somewhere. This betting site, with the three of you, proves that they are collecting real money, through actual money gateways. That's unheard of. Everything we have come across earlier was strictly in Bitcoins and low value. Location, killer, transactions, everything falls in unknown country, unknown jurisdiction…'

Raghav spoke, '…and of course, Khurana was an investigating government officer… So, they would have to share, that's kind of an unwritten code.'

Vikram inwardly smirks, Raghav is welcome to his delusions. There is neither honour nor righteousness in this soulless place. They want the exact same thing that we want: information. We are mere hounds sent out with a whiff of tantalizing smells, to hit the trails they cannot be seen walking.

Smith asks, 'What about the faces in Zameer's and Khurana's videos?'

Vikram responds, 'Dr Nicole Augusto, the face in Zameer's video, is a trained psychiatrist. She has an alibi during Zameer's killing. She was with us during Suraj Singh and Khurana's killing. We are her alibi. Tashi, the face in Khurana's killing, she is my deputy and forensic expert. She was in the office, on duty, when Khurana was killed.'

Smith nods, 'Interesting. She planted you guys at the crime scene, created suspects, then got you guys to become each other's alibis and cancel out each other… Tell me, Mr Vikram, did these deputies of yours, Tashi and Mr Khurana, have anything going on between them?'

Vikram laughs, 'Hell no, absolutely not, she couldn't stand the prick.'

'How can you know…?'

Vikram is quick to reply, 'In fact, that could be the reason

Khurana fell for it. He was flattered that the woman who had shown him such disdain secretly wanted to fuck him.'

A few moments of silence descend. Each man inwardly recognizing the truth in that statement.

She was creating an extremely tangled web. A web that Vikram could feel tightening around himself, even as they chatted and sipped tea.

This unmarked enclave that he had been granted entry into, had more dirty secrets than his little mind could ever comprehend. The warm winter sun that was bathing them was meaningless in front of the dark cold calculations that saw only data, not human beings. Poor Khurana had become mere data.

'Why is the killer so sure of getting away? There is so much… activity. Bidders are bidding on the site. They know when to bid, where to go to see the killing… The killer is reaching out to them in some way. There is so much happening. Why can't it be traced? There must be several people involved.' Raghav's question seems pertinent.

Vikram replies, 'Of course there are. The operation is probably broken into a dozen smaller jobs. The teams working on it could be living in different parts of the world. Individuals, who have never met each other, don't know about each other, who probably don't even know the final use of what they are creating. That information lies only with the killer.'

Smith adds, 'And the kill-film website data is getting deleted instantaneously.'

'I thought nothing ever gets deleted from the net.' Raghav asks.

'What exactly is happening?' Vikram looks at Smith.

'By delete, I don't mean it is erased.' Smith replies. 'In fact, quite the opposite. CMND-Z blocked. That's what we call it. That the data moves in an encrypted format is a given. Encryptions have a key with which you can retrieve it. This takes it further. This data is not meant to be recovered ever. So the site is programmed to garble itself perpetually. Within minutes, it's so far gone that retrieving it, reconstituting it in its original form is only theoretically possible, in reality, it cannot be done.

'The source is camouflaged by bouncing it across IP addresses. By the time it appeared, it had bounced around thousands of times and will continue to do so for…don't know how long. And if we do crack the source, which we will eventually, it will be a dead end anyway.

'All the websites we found so far operate in the same way. So there is no way to know where and by whom it was uploaded, who paid, to which bank, who received…What we are passing on to you are internal screen recordings taken by our built-in recorders. By now, this betting website, with you guys in it, will be so far garbled that it will be unrecognizable. Even if we locate it today, it will not stand up in any court as evidence.'

Vikram digests this, there is a visible gloom settled over him. It's like a door has been slammed on his face. He had been hoping to get a glimpse at the source, depending on it to give him some clues. 'She's made the style of killing into a signature, she has turned herself into a fucking…'

'…brand!' Smith completes it for him. 'The reason this meeting was granted…it came up four hours ago.'

He opens up another bidding site. It is similar to the first one, with some critical changes. Khurana has been removed from the gallery, Raghav has been added. Vikram bursts out into genuine laughter, 'So that's the reason I am here, your butt's on fire, finally!'

Raghav scowls.

Vikram's picture has changed. It's more flattering than the

earlier one. He looks kind of rakishly charming. He has three million euros against his name already, while Raghav has a mere fifty thousand. Tashi has one million euros.

'Or is it the fact that I am a hotter bet than you?' Vikram taunts.

Smith watches Vikram closely. For a man with one dead deputy, one under suspicion…and the killer's count down ticking against his own name, he is too damn cool.

Vikram understands why he is sitting on the perfectly manicured lawn, sipping tea with Smith. Now, he is both the hound and the rabbit. His mobile phone, handed over at the entrance, would have given away his digital life even as he tried to dig for information in this fortress. Well, they were in for a surprise, an alarm bell had gone off in his head that morning when Raghav called to demand his immediate presence. 'We have been called over by the source,' he had said.

As a result, Vikram's neighbour's kid had made a thousand bucks for lending Vikram his mobile for a day. Smith gets a message. Vikram's phone has yielded nothing but an eleven-year-old's gibberish.

Smith gets to his feet, 'Well gentlemen, it was interesting meeting you.'

As Vikram and Raghav walk out back into the street, Vikram laughs silently, 'Screw you bastards, GQH…C…or whatever clutch of letters you concoct to name yourself. You don't get me so easily.'

As they get into Raghav's official car, both switch on their mobiles. Vikram scrolls though the calls, recent activity, messages… contacts. A single ten-digit number has been added. Smith's calling card, he presumes correctly.

28

Eeky

Interior of Vikram's office.

The previous night's search had brought forth four possible suspects. Nicole and Tashi spread out the carefully categorized material on them. Khurana's absence is like a gaping hole none is acknowledging.

A young man walks in. He could be a clone of Khurana's. Vikram and Nicole stare at him.

Tashi is about to make the introductions. Vikram cuts in, 'Let me guess, Raghav has assigned you to be my new pain in the butt.'

The man decides to swallow his reply. Tashi almost feels sorry for him. 'This is Sanjeev Malhotra,' she makes the introduction.

Nicole starts briefing everyone, 'Four suspects on our list, their life stories kind of match, so does the age group and body type. I have voice samples, contacts and photos for these two—Kartikeya Nair and Shruti Kher.'

Tashi has their pictures up, comparing them with the killer's body in the video. The body types seem similar, give or take, five to six-kilo difference.

Nicole continues, 'The third suspect. Farzana B—strong personality, borderline nymphomaniac, lived in different parts of the world. She was part of a rock band. She dropped out of therapy. No photo, but DNA testing possible.'

She opens a file labelled Farzana B, pulls out an envelope. She empties its contents on a sheet of paper. Something rolls out.

'What the fuck is that?' Vikram asks.

'A tooth with a diamond embedded in it.'

Vikram picks it up with his all-purpose tweezers, the one he used earlier to remove mushrooms from his pizza. The embedded diamond is indeed a work of art if one is into that kind of thing.

'Extracting it and leaving it behind with me was her way of declaring that she was leaving behind the delusionary lifestyle she had lived for a decade.' Nicole informs.

Next, she puts on the table a folded sheet of handmade organic paper. 'Rossane Singh. Suffered periodic episodes of hallucinations since childhood. I suspected it to be the result of some trauma that she couldn't recollect. Left this for me during our last session.'

Vikram opens the folded sheet of paper. Discovers an exotic, blue-green dyed hair arrangement inside. It's quirky, yet eye-catching. Nicole answers his unasked question, 'Rossane's hair for sure, she had coloured it.'

Next, he holds the paper against the light, observes the writing on the paper closely. The red colour of the ink has spread into the organic paper filaments, almost like blood in vein and arteries.

Vikram reads aloud: 'To my only friend in the world, for the things that could have been, but never will be. I will miss you. ...heavy stuff. Is this blood?'

'I don't know, it felt … eeky. So I kind of never touched it.'

Tashi seals it all into separate bags and heads with Malhotra for the lab.

'We are all very fragile Vikram, we are all a little crazy in our own way. Sometimes just a little nudge is enough to push a person over the edge.' Nicole says softly.

Vikram looks at her for an extended moment, she is holding so much inside her. The pain that her patients poured in front of her, didn't all just slide away. Some of it clung to her, a burden she is still carrying for them.

Vikram decides it's time to set her free, 'You have given us what we need. As we investigate deeper into these women, there could be a backlash. I want you to be very careful. Do not go anywhere or do anything that is out of your routine. Be suspicious of every new person who comes your way.'

Nicole realizes that her job here is done, she seems quite relieved. Vikram cautions, 'Most important, do not mention it to anybody…about what you did for us. Contact us immediately if anything out of routine happens. Do not come here again. We will contact you only if needed.'

Vikram puts his arm around her shoulder and gently leads her to the door, his fingers graze the bare skin of her arm. With a half grateful smile, she walks away. Vikram realizes that this was the first time he actually touched her. He runs his thumb over his fingers, almost expecting to touch her again. Then watches her as she walks away, her image getting slowly disfigured and distant as she passes through a series of distorting glass partitions in the outer office.

He is brought back to the present with a sharp sound. An agitated Tashi has dumped a lab report file on the table. She is quoting from it.

'It says here "very mild traces of sedative in sandwich mustard sauce sample…" You did a test on my Subway sandwich wrapper? You thought I could be faking my sleep! You seriously thought it could have been me making out with Khurana?'

Vikram shrugs, 'It was your face in the video. I had to check you…you know that.' He reads the report. 'And now we find out someone ensured you would fall asleep. Who got the food?'

'Khurana did.'

'He wouldn't have sedated you if he was waiting for a late

night hot date with you.'

'Slipping in a roofie would have been more his style,' she snorts.

Vikram is thoughtful then gives her precise instructions. 'Tracking down the four women on the list is an absolute priority. Keep an escort with you always. Remember, you are also on the bidding site. Nicole is to be left out of all further investigations.'

Tashi nods, then comes back with a final outburst, 'Honestly, me with Khurana? How could you? If nothing else, you could have at least credited me with better taste in men.'

Slam. She is gone. Vikram is amused. Women! She was angry with him for suspecting her of making out with Khurana...not for killing him!

29

Bonded

It is night outside. Vikram heads for the Subway joint Khurana must have picked the sandwich from. It's just a regular busy joint. He buys a sandwich, studies it.

He visualizes how easy it would be for anybody to spike the sandwich with a simple disposable syringe filled with liquid sedative. A tiny hole in the paper packing would be practically invisible. And the sharp mustard taste would have disguised anything. He chucks the sandwich uneaten into a waste bin.

Then he buys a bouquet of flowers and heads for the hospital across the road. He makes his way through the busy corridors to the door at the back, leading to a large room.

Anand is talking softly with a distinguished-looking man, Dr Bhatia. A nurse is hovering in the background. On the bed is a shrivelled comatose figure of a woman on a life support system. She is so far gone that she hardly looks human.

The room is uncharacteristically alive. Paintings, books, pictures of her and Vikram together, with their parents, with Anand. They tell the story of the woman on the bed. She is Vikram's twin sister, Vidya.

Anand's fiancée, Vidya.

Vikram enters, places the flowers in a vase. 'It's five years today, we'd agreed on a re-think...' Anand begins.

Vikram is moving about as though he can't hear a word. He heads for the bed. Takes the bony hand in his, nudges and pulls playfully at the fingers, willing them to respond. To him, Anand's voice is now an indecipherable drone in the background.

He sits on the steel stool next to the bed. He has completely blocked out everybody.

Anand takes a long last look at Vidya. Then he and Dr Bhatia leave.

'Let him take as long as he needs. My son and I owe him so much...' Dr Bhatia says.

Anand sits in the chair right outside the door, waits. His eyes reflect a blankness that has come after years of pain and loss.

Vikram remains hunched over his sister, as still as her.

Anand opens his eyes. He had fallen asleep on the seat. It's just past dawn. Vikram is looking down at him, 'Vidya and I began life together...our breaths were in sync... I somehow believed we would...go together... and now, it is my destiny to kill her...'

Anand, still groggy, blurts out, 'You aren't killing her Vikram... You kept her alive... She would have wanted this...you need to start anew... you...'

But Vikram didn't hear him. He signs on some papers, places them next to Anand and walks away. It is his authorization to take Vidya off the life support system. Anand knows what they are and is unable to look at them.

Had Vidya met with the accident three weeks later, she and Anand would have been married. He would have been her husband, not her boyfriend. It would have been his signature on the papers. He had been spared the unbearable burden that Vikram would have to carry all his life. That thought crushes him and the tears that had been held back for years, stream down his cheeks into his shaggy beard.

The medical staff moves in to detach the life support system.

He can hear rising whispers. They have discovered that Vikram had already disconnected the life support system, Vidya is already dead. Anand realizes that Vikram actually meant it when he said he had killed her.

The nurse looks askance at Dr Bhatia, he just nods, then signs off, declaring the procedure is complete.

30

Father

Vikram walks out of the hospital. The streets are still empty, he strolls into a nearby park.

He picks some stale bread lying next to a sleeping tramp, tucks a fifty rupee note under his head. He crumbles the hard bread and spreads it on the grass for the birds to feed on. No birds came. He sits on a park bench and lets his head drop back. As the day brightens, his heavy eyes droop into a dark sleep.

A crazy mixed up, disjointed dream, grabs hold of him almost instantaneously. He sees Vidya in the hospital. His fingers are caught in the tangle of tubes from her life support system. Then he sees himself with the killer, she is on top of him, her finger's feel like daggers on his chest and neck as she probes and caresses. Her head thrown back, her face is obliterated by blinding sunlight. He is trying to call out, he can't. He is trying to stop his hand from disconnecting the ventilator in the hospital, he can't. Now, he can see the face of the killer as she dramatically lowers her head and locks her eyes with his. The face of the killer is Nicole, then Tashi, sometimes Rumana, sometimes himself. The maid and the pugs are mixed in it somehow. The sun is burning in his eyes. He is choking…choking…and then it is Khurana on top of him…

Vikram wakes up thrashing with a coughing fit. He is still on the park bench.

The fat young boy is shaking him vigorously, 'I want to be there when you find her. I want to be there.'

'You fucking psycho, get away from me.' He pushes the boy away with all his strength, gets to his feet and starts walking away.

Vikram is still a bit disorientated. The boy is still pursuing him, constantly in his space.

'You have to promise me, you have to,' He keeps repeating.

Vikram tries to push him away, but can't. The rock-like strength of the youngster and his steel grip makes Vikram stop. This was not the strength he expected from this over-sized soft looking body. He has no choice but to stop.

'Zameer was my dad. I want to see the film,' the boy blurts. This has Vikram's attention. The young boy instantly lets go of the grip, takes a step back.

Back in the screening room.

Vikram is on the phone. Raghav is at the other end, 'Yes, he is Zameer's son, Michael Paddington, British mother. A rather well-kept secret.'

Vikram nods at Tashi, she starts the film.

Vikram's complete focus is on Michael. He studies the boy's response closely. He watches the tremors running through his body. He watches him sink into the chair, the soft sob, the choking sound as though he had been hit, blow after blow.

Film over, Michael doubles up and dry retches over and over again, as though something inside is trying to come out violently but not being able to.

To Michael, that was not Zameer, it was not a sex kill. It was just his dad. The dad who never cared to even acknowledge his existence. The dad he would never know. He is crying uncontrollably now. He is just a large over-grown child.

This unwanted son's undisguised misery and pain suddenly make Zameer Khan 'real' for Tashi. She sits down on the floor beside him and holds him. She averts her face, not wanting either Vikram or Michael to see the tears in her own eyes. Tears of empathy and shame. Shame at having become so hardened by her world that she had allowed a young son to face what no son should ever have to endure.

The ache that love and death brings, weighs heavily on Vikram too. He sits down in a chair, facing away from them. The shadow of his sister's death is back on his face. By now, Anand would have cremated her. By now, she would be mere ashes flying in the wind. By now… His mobile phone starts vibrating. He ignores it, the vibration continues. He answers.

'Can I see the film again?' It was Anand.

Vikram explodes, 'Do you think I run a fucking multiplex with several shows a day?'

31

Testing Times

Back home, in the living room.

Anand arranges a full-size male silicon dummy on the floor. He discreetly searches Vikram's face for the pain and bereavement. Vikram's face is a hard mask now; all his attention focused on the dummy. Anand recognizes that empathy is not welcome, some men don't cry; they connect differently. He gets business-like.

The dummy is as near a real body as can be. Bones, muscles, nerve centres, internal organs, everything.

Vikram plays Khurana's video on the wall-mounted television. Anand adjusts the dummy on the floor and is about to squat on it like the killer. Suddenly, Vikram understands what he is up to. Pushing him aside, Vikram straddles the dummy and replicates the killer's hits as closely as he can. It's almost like a segment of his dream.

Anand nods, 'That's right, she wasn't hitting randomly. She knew just where to hit.'

Vikram muses, 'When she pretends to caress the man, she is actually probing, searching for the nerve points, organs. She locates them, memorizes them and hits when the time is right.'

He replicates her caresses on the torso and at the same time tries to probe for nerve points.

Anand tells him, 'That's not easy. For each of us, the exact pressure point will be a few millimetres off. You will never get it right the first time. With each hit, she paralyzed a different part of the body, created a different type of pain.'

'So, she is a doctor?'

Anand shrugs, 'She knows the human body really well. Masseuse, physiotherapist, forensic expert, martial arts...lots of disciplines teach you.'

For Vikram, a whole new door has opened.

A few hours later.

Two experts have been brought into the screening room. They watch the films with the faces blurred out. Then replicate the moves on several separate dummies.

The dummies are rigged to a strength monitor that churns out reports of the exact location and strength of each hit. It also indicates the possible paralyzing impact on the body. Each expert needs several tries before getting the spots and strength correct for the entire series. Yet, she had done it so effortlessly.

The first expert, Tej Wadia, is a reed-thin sixty-year-old and has the look of an ascetic. An acclaimed kung fu teacher, inspired by the great Bruce Lee himself. He in turn, had inspired a generation of students. Tej gives his opinion, 'These hits are impressive but her big move is flipping the man over... She looks just about sixty kilos, and the men look closer to eighty. Full weight pinning down on her.'

Emanuel Lobo, the second expert, a retired wrestler and chiropractor by profession, points out, 'Look at how she adjusts the man's body so that his centre of gravity aligns with the centre of her hips.'

As each move is described, the actual sequence of movements in each killing is playing out on the screens. What looked like sexual responses, get re-interpreted now, as a martial arts expert's preparatory actions.

Lobo continues his analysis, '... and here, when she lifts her hips to meet his downward thrust, she is checking his weight...'

Sure enough, her upward pelvic thrusts are nothing but tests to check if she can lift the men.

Wadia elaborates, 'That flip-over is a very tough move and could have cracked her backbone, but she was confident of pulling it off...'

For Vikram, the information is coming in so rapidly, it's re-orienting his entire approach.

He adjusts all the videos on the screen to a single moment, when her palms made contact with their lower back—Zameer Khan, Khurana and Suraj Singh—all frozen in time, in almost identical postures.

Vikram marks the point of contact on the screen, 'She grabbed each one here, at the base of the spine, near the tailbone area, moments before the flip. Each man responded in the same way.'

'It is after this that all the actions follow the killing-rhythm, this seems to be the starting.' Tej agrees.

Vikram marks the base of the spine on the silicon dummy. 'What is here? What could she have done?' he asks.

Anand is scratching his head.

Shekhar plays all the three films, frame by frame. Her actions match with amazing precision in all of them. The darkness in Khurana and Suraj's films make it impossible to observe the details. But Zameer's film shows a miniature flash just under her right palm. It lasts for just two frames. Magnified ten times over, it reveals more secrets.

Zameer was pinning her down with his full body weight. She wrapped her legs around him, pulling him even closer. It permitted her to get her hands behind his back. That's when the diamond fangs on her bracelet disappeared...then reappeared. They are now held between the index and middle fingers of each hand. They are visible for just two frames as her hands come down with the fangs pointed in the direction of the base of the spine. Pulling him closer was not an erotic act. It allowed her to plunge the hair-breadth thin razor-sharp diamond fangs into the base of his spine.

'That's it!' Anand exclaims. 'She punctured the nerves in the lumbar area, maybe even injected something, probably paralyzing his hips and quadriceps in some way, caused him to freeze and loosen his grip on her lower body.'

On-screen, from this perspective, Zameer's response makes sense.

Vikram observes, 'His upper body arched, what we mistook for a sexual response is an acute shock and pain. His thighs loosened their grip on her hips. That permitted her to execute her manoeuvre of turning him around and getting on top. Now, she has him pinned down.'

'Once she had his lower body paralyzed, then the upper body blows must have paralyzed the entire body, making all retaliation impossible for the man.' Lobo confirms.

Vikram asks, 'The ripping of the jugular, what is that move called?'

The two experts try the jab again and again on the dummy. They simply end up squashing the neck. Tej steps back, 'In my forty-five years of practising kung fu, with my bare hands I have broken many bones, torn muscles and ligaments, punctured internal organs but always as internal injuries. Never have my fingers penetrated flesh...yet she has done it effortlessly.'

Lobo adds, 'It's a killer's deliberate move. Her training is so specialized that there can't be too many practitioners across the world. There can't be too many teachers either.'

Vikram is looking at the videos with barely concealed

excitement. She is a challenge that just keeps expanding. In his mind, he is trying to make it happen to himself, trying to search for a clue... He is facing a truly incredible human being and it makes him feel alive.

For the first time, the shadow that was clinging to him after Vidya's death seems to be receding. There is a rising twinkle in his eyes. He finds himself smiling.

Then it hits him.

Shit! She has honey-trapped him already! Would he be ready to go off with her if she were to appear before him right now? Yes, he would. He is not looking for clues, he is imagining being fucked by her. Right now, she had made him as easy as Khurana had been. Moron...

32

Past Continuous

Vikram makes a call, to his buddy, Detective Katsuru in Japan.

Katsuru is amused, 'Ah! The she-killer who fucks then kills with her bare hands. That is the story of every manga comic heroine I have ever read...'

Vikram cuts in, 'Can you help?'

'No, but maybe my old uncle, the Dai-Osho can.'

'Great, put him on conference.'

Katsuru laughs, 'You must be joking! I have to do it in person with proper respect. He is ninety-seven years old, bachelor monk high priest Dai-Osho... A man of few words.'

Vikram wonders how Katsuru plans to respectfully show the Dai-Osho the snuff porn. Oh well, let Katsuru sort it out. Now he has to wait.

Vikram gets a video call from Katsuru. He is sitting respectfully next to a very ancient-looking abbot with an inscrutable face. He is holding an iPad for the Dai Osho to watch the killings. The old man watches in silence with hooded eyes. Vikram is watching the Dai-Osho closely, waiting to read some response from him.

The Dai-Osho speaks briefly in Japanese. Katsuru translates, 'I cannot say what it is. I cannot help you.'

Katsuru bows repeatedly and is about to cut the call.

'Hey wait.' Vikram stops him. 'Does that mean the old man doesn't know or won't tell?'

Katsuru's eyes widen in alarm at this grave disrespect towards the Dai-Osho. He disconnects in a hurry.

Vikram is left with a deep feeling of discontent. Something was telling him that the old man knew...something. His mobile phone vibrates, a message from Tashi. 'Archives, urgent.'

He reaches the central government's archives. Rows of shelves piled with books. Hundreds of shelves that haven't been touched for decades. In the dusty sunlight, he sees a strange sight.

A woman, practising hand movements, flicks and jabs, almost like exotic dance mudras, they are strangely familiar. He moves closer.

It's Tashi with several open books spread on a table. She is replicating some of the stances and exercises from the sketches in front of her. Tashi laughs when she sees the amusement on Vikram's face, 'Which girl doesn't want to ride her man and make him beg for mercy?'

He spies Michael at the end of the row of shelves. Tashi notices his gaze, 'It was his idea. He is training to be a sumo wrestler.'

For Vikram, the strength, grip and stance that he had noticed in the boy's movements suddenly make sense. 'We saw a violent porn star killer, he saw a master at work,' she says.

Vikram watches the boy, there is a silent determination about him. He admits ruefully, 'Our eyes are closed even when we believe them to be open. He saw past the titillation and sex, the very first time. He saw only pain, attack and death.'

Michael walks over with a couple of reference books. Opens pages revealing a series of sketches, charcoal drawings, illustrations and instructions. Some of the sketches mirror the frozen frames of the killer's arm position before the lethal jab.

His voice has a controlled excitement in it, 'Check this out. The only translation of the Japanese traveller Miyo Yamaguchi, late sixteen century. He mentions a deadly art form that was developed by a sect of samurais. These men went into battle empty-handed and were deeply feared.'

Vikram is already scanning the pages with his phone, 'Any idea if it's still taught?'

Tashi is rapid reading, 'Nothing.'

Vikram draws Tashi aside, 'What news on the four suspects from Nicole's list?'

'Suspect number one, Kartikeya Nair died two years ago of a childhood cardiac condition, number two, Shruti Kher is happily married and eight months pregnant, that rules her out. Number three and four; waiting for the DNA results. I heard about your sister, I'm sorry ...if there is anything I can...'

Vikram barely nods then turns away. She watches as he walks away, it's like he is receding into something...deep... She can't figure it out. He disappears around a bookshelf.

Vikram suddenly stops, 'Hey, the escort I ordered...' A man steps out from the next series of shelves. The escort. He nods at Vikram then steps out of view again. Vikram leaves.

He is wondering how Tashi knew about his sister. From Anand, of course. Well, he would never have guessed the two of them could have anything in common.

33

Abbot

Early morning.

A flight takes off with Vikram on board. Flies into the rising sun—Japan.

Katsuru is waiting for him at the gate of the ancient temple garden. He is not looking forward to meeting the Dai-Osho again. But he is looking forward to meeting his old friend.

Vikram gets off the cab and marches straight past him and into the temple gate.

Katsuru cribs, 'Hey, what's the hurry? Haven't seen you in… like four years.'

Vikram comes back impatiently, pumps his hand, gives him a brisk hug, 'What four years? We saw each other just two days ago. Come on, move it.'

Armed with images of the drawings and scrolls from the archives, Vikram and a reluctant Katsuru head inside. Seeing the Dai-Osho in person, Vikram understands Katsuru's respectful demeanour.

The Dai-Osho is seated on a low seat. He is very weak, almost fading away. He looks so ancient…almost like from another age. Vikram feels a tinge of pathos seeing the old man.

Katsuru respectfully explains Vikram's quest once again to the Dai-Osho and lays out the images on the floor. The old man doesn't glance up. Vikram is not even sure if he has heard Katsuru's long explanation.

'Tell him I know it existed for several centuries; I need to know who practices it now, where is it taught…'

Katsuru rapidly translates. The only response they get sounds like a snore. Vikram is getting really impatient now.

'Tell him three are dead already and there could be a fourth killing even as we talk. So if he knows something and is not telling, this one is on his conscience, not mine.'

Katsuru is stung, but translates a diluted version anyway.

The Dai-Osho stirs ever so slightly, makes a subtle signal with his fingers. A young monk rushes to him with a pot of ink and a scroll of paper.

Painstakingly, the Dai-Osho draws on it, the wrist does a slow dance leaving behind beautiful strokes. It's not letters of the alphabet, it's not words. It is the figure of a strange beast, neither wolf nor tiger, that seems to have formed from some vapour and is roaring at the invisible sky. It emanates a stillness and controlled violence. Vikram can't take his eyes off it. He's seen it before… but can't put his finger on it.

The last stroke in place, the old man recedes into stillness.

Vikram is puzzled. What in the world is the meaning of the drawing? Why does it look familiar? It looks like a super cool post-apocalypse mutant demon.

Katsuru recognizes the image, 'Garou. A demon wolf with an appetite for destruction! Very popular image in the tattoo parlours. My son's basketball team mascot.'

The Dai-Osho sighs and gives Katsuru a look that shrivels him, then speaks in a whisper, 'Garou. It was the secret name of a deeply respected combat philosophy of the old ages.'

Vikram is taken aback. The Dai-Osho replied not in Japanese but in halting rustic Bihari Hindi.

The Dai-Osho continues, 'It was perfect for an age when the

warrior had no option but to kill or be killed. Sheer brutality and insistence on the death of the opponent, even amongst students at the end of the training session... The rules were so uncompromising that a master managed to graduate just a handful of students in an entire lifetime. The very quality that made its practitioner a respected warrior in the olden days...made it unsuitable for the civilized world... And so it had been banished.'

Vikram knows better, 'But, obviously it did not remain banished...'

'Shiro, he was a stubborn man, one of the last surviving practitioners with the spirit of the Garou,' the Dai-Osho adds. 'He believed that without the experience of death a true warrior student was never complete. He believed that only death can be the culmination for a duel. Just like in nature, strife is constant, combat is constant; it only ends when one of the two dies. "The world is a big place, and the true student will come drawn to the true master," that's what he said.'

Silence returns to the garden. A little bird hops close to the Dai-Osho, so close. Then on to the trailing hem of his robe, unaware of the human presence just centimetres away. Vikram watches, fascinated at the abbot's complete stillness.

The Dai-Osho speaks again, 'He had made the slopes of Mount Kilauea in Hawaii his home.'

Katsuru begins excitedly, 'That's an active volcano...'

'Just like him...' the Dai-Osho adds. Then gives Vikram an enigmatic long look. The ancient clouded eyes seem to penetrate to his very soul.

'What are you searching for?' he asks.

It's clear he is asking Vikram something totally unrelated to his visible quest for the killer. It unnerves Vikram. He doesn't want to face what the ancient wisdom sees. To cover it up he asks, 'Your Hindi…'

'Bodhgaya…I was a young boy then…'

He falls back into silence. The wind whistles in the bamboo grove, somewhere, bells tinkle. Vikram and Katsuru start moving away. Unexpectedly, the Dai-Osho laughs, a loud whole-hearted laugh, his face lights up, his eyes twinkle.

'Basketball team mascot you say? Perhaps, it is better this way, let the old be wiped out and the young find new meaning.'

34

The Passing

Vikram enters his house. An Indian premier league cricket match is playing on the sports channel. Over the breathless high pitch commentary, Anand is frozen mid-action, he is demonstrating a batting stroke to Tashi. He is clean-shaven, almost unrecognizable. Without the bushy growth, he is a good-looking man.

She is stretched out on the sofa, eating a bowl of noodles, wearing Anand's T-shirt. Seeing Vikram makes Anand seethe. 'New rule, you…you… can't keep your mobile off.'

Tashi looks at Vikram, 'We've been calling you for three days, your calls were diverted to an answering machine; we were worried.'

Vikram is silent. He is watching the two of them, their easy body language with each other tells him a lot. Anand's shaven face tells him even more.

'You were the highest bid on her betting site…' Tashi reminds him.

Vikram nods vaguely and pretends to be preoccupied. He enters his room and closes the door behind him. Anand has moved on, left Vidya behind. Five years is a long wait for any man, Anand had done it for his Vidya.

Vikram finds himself in front of the mirror, averts his gaze. He had stopped shaving his head the day she died, now the stubble covered his head, marking a clear hairline. Even as she lived, they had both been grieving for five long years, and now with her dead… He is struggling to wish his friend well, but he can't get the black hole in his heart to go away. His shoulders sink, he allows himself to flop on the bed, stares into the darkness.

Anand picks up his glass and pretends to make his way to the kitchen. He stops in front of Vikram's closed door. He can't get himself to knock. His face reflects the exact same darkness as Vikram's.

Vikram becomes aware of the shadow blocking the streak of light that peeps in from under his door. He knows it is Anand. Unable to come in or turn away. Anand steps back, then goes to the kitchen and pours a drink he doesn't want. Something has passed out of their lives forever.

35

Whirr

Next day. Vikram's office.

Vikram enters to find Tashi and Malhotra peering over a laptop.

Tashi is actually smiling, 'Take a look.'

He squints down at the screen and sees images of two hair samples in microscopic detail. The images reveal identical patterns in both the hair samples. 'What am I looking at?'

Tashi explains, 'This on the right is the hair we found on the beach and this on the left is Rossane's hair from Nicole's records.'

Vikram nods and sits down to have a closer look. Tashi points at identical gaps in both the hair. 'The identical gaps… Pilaianulace, a very rare hair condition. It showed up in the hair on the beach. It's in Rossane's hair too. The chance of it turning up in hair belonging to two different women is… really rare. So, even though the DNA results are not in, I believe it has to be her. And your suspicion was correct, the writing on the paper, it is blood.'

Vikram sits back. So, finally, they have a suspect and material evidence. 'Rossanne… What do we know about her?'

Malhotra pipes in, 'She is a US citizen. Immigration records show that three years ago, she returned to the US, which was just two months after she stopped treatment with Nicole.'

'So where is she now?'

'No record of her leaving the country since then. I contacted her brother, her only living relative. He said they have been estranged for nearly a decade. Middle-aged Silicon Valley type, a complete contrast to her. He didn't really give a damn about her, in fact, he seemed quite relieved to say he knew nothing about her!'

'So, as of now, she is untraceable?' Vikram asks.

Tashi replies, 'Kind of. We pulled out a picture from old immigration records.'

Malhotra places an image of Rossane's passport before him. Vikram studies her face and scowls. It's an unflattering mugshot, a narrow angular face with a sharp hooked nose, small eyes with dark circles and low hairline. It's quite evident that it would take a lot to make her a beauty.

Tashi can read his scowl and silently agrees with him. Rossane's is not a face that Zameer Khan would go anywhere near. Malhotra pulls out a full-length image that reveals her body frame to be at least fifteen pounds heavier than the killer in the film. Vikram frowns deeper and scratches his stubbly head.

Tashi is not going to give up hope, after all, the hair matched. 'Body sculpting happens at every street corner these days. Nose, eyes, lips, boobs, butt…everything is on sale…it's really not that difficult…' she says. She resizes the image on the laptop to make it look leaner. The face also squashes, giving Rossane a comical hawk-like profile. Tashi quickly undoes it.

Vikram is staring at the letter with the blood ink. He turns it over and over against the light streaming in from the window. Macabre though it is, there is an unmistakable beauty in the calligraphy. The stroke of each alphabet flows gracefully into the next. There is a barely visible watermark at the bottom left corner. The watermark has been designed to look like a wave that's transforming into a cloud. Very distinctive. Next to it is the name of a famous art gallery in the city, The Zone.

Vikram reaches The Zone. In the entrance foyer is a large sculpture that matches the symbol in the watermark on the paper. It's been many years since he climbed the once familiar steps.

He was nineteen and working hard to hook up with an art student. Simone was four years older than him. The Googled 'gyan' he sprouted to impress her was alternately amusing and irritating.

She, in turn, was expending her energies to hook up with an artist nearly two decades older than her. One day, Vikram saw himself reflected in her futile efforts to impress the artist. It made him squirm. He quit.

The interiors had been completely redone and he has to check the signboard to find the stationery shop. He holds up the paper for the sales lady to see. She nods, 'That's ours.' She points towards an entire shelf that has boxes of identical paper on sale. 'It's handmade with recycled jute bags by artisans in Bengal. Try it. It's been our most popular item for years. We regularly export…'

Vikram cuts her sales pitch by flashing his photo Id. He places a copy of Rossane picture on the counter. 'Rossane Singh. Do you know her? Has she ever had an exhibition here? Worked here? Attended classes, workshops?'

Some of the other salesgirls take a peek at the picture. Nobody recognizes her. 'I'll check the records for the name. Our data goes back over a decade. If she is connected with the gallery in any way, she will show up. It will take some time,' says the clerk.

Vikram nods. The persistent saleslady is about to restart her monologue, 'In the meantime, maybe I could show you some of…' He heads out to the exhibit area.

He strolls through the gallery. It is a hall full of paintings. 'Hunger' the banner at the entrance shrieks. Vikram gives it a pass. But it does remind him that he hasn't eaten for a bit. He buys a sandwich at the cafeteria. The clerk at the counter suggests, 'Maybe you would like to try our fresh cheese quiches, homemade cheese from Pondicherry…'

He ignores the lady and parks himself at the farthest table facing a blank wall. Vikram always believed it helped him think, a blank space is full of possibilities. A large group of noisy tourists walks in, led by a really loud guide. Within a minute, the cafeteria sounds worse than a fish market at peak hour. Vikram rapidly exits.

He needs silence, he needs to think. The whole Rossane possibility has not fully sunk into him as yet. The face in Zameer's eyes, Nicole's face, is haunting him. In all the days she spent with them, he never saw the same quality in Nicole's face. And no matter how much he stretches his imagination, he can't see it in Rossane's face either.

In Rumana Dhawan, he had seen traces of it. He could still feel the heat of her presence. Her darting tongue reaching for his earlobe. Why the fuck did she have so many convenient alibis. Convenient alibis, just the way they had found the hair on the beach. A 'convenient' clue? Was it really convenient? They could have easily missed it.

He finds a quiet corner behind a large canvas partition. The section has been cordoned off with a small barricade that he absent-mindedly crossed. Now, perched on some unopened boxes, he allows himself to ruminate in peace.

A soft persistent mechanical *whirr* makes its presence felt. He looks around for its origin. Some men are at work, probably setting up for a new exhibition. The sound is coming from a long mechanical arm that's moving back and forth on a kind of contoured mesh.

Intrigued, he walks over. A 3D art installation is being created.

The moving mechanical arm is depositing the precise amount of silicon on the contoured mesh. The mesh is perched on a grid two feet above the ground. An artist is bending over it precariously, studying the process.

As the silicon dries, the shapes get sharpened. It's a series of multidimensional faces entwined into each other. It is fascinating in a grotesque sort of way.

'What is this? he asks.

'Faces, I call it,' the artist replies.

'Great choice, but what…is this thing?'

The artist responds with barely concealed pride in his voice, 'My custom-made 3D printer, the only one of its kind in the world, at four square inches a minute, it's the only…'

Vikram can't help wondering, for an art gallery, everyone here sounded like a salesman. Even as the silicon dries, the artist starts air-spraying a skin colour on them, instantly, the silicon film starts looking like skin. He is fascinated. He walks around the frame studying the faces from all angles. Each face has been positioned so ingeniously that no matter where he goes, there seems to be a face always turned towards him. Faces do seem to have taken up his life recently.

The artist is still talking, 'This here… I am recreating my original installation from my art gallery in New York.'

'I don't get it.'

'I mapped every detail of my original installation and fed the information into this beauty here, just like you do in an ordinary printer. The original took me three years to make, it is made of multiple alloys. This 3D printer will have the silicon replica ready in a matter of hours. It is meant to last for just a few weeks, it decays and falls apart after that. It disfigures easily, stretches, bends… Have to be careful…have to…'

Vikram is becoming aware something important is being said to him.

'…So I used silicon in the 3D printer to create this. Viola! I have a perfect replica.'

'A perfect replica?'

'Each time.'

'Each time?'

'Yes, now my original does not travel, only this printer and the dismantle-able mesh travels with me, across the world, recreating. This is changing the way art works, the way artist work, it's huge, it's….

'So, each time, you get the same result?' Vikram interrupts. The artist nods, 'And sometimes, better than the original.' He winks. 'The printer does for me the stuff that I can't do with my hands in the original.'

'Isn't that cheating? They come here to see your work, the original.'

'This is my work, I am, uh…re-interpreting it, so, it's original.'

'And when you need to do something different?'

Vikram is now flat on the ground and peering under the grid.

'This printer holds seven different programmes on it. I can choose anything from the menu. I can recreate any of my seven most popular installations in a jiffy any time I want,' the artist preens.

Before he can be stopped, Vikram slips under the grid and is lying beneath it. The artist is flattered by his interest and is still talking. Once again, Vikram has switched off. He is only aware of the grid and the printer arm above him.

He watches the arm sweep over him, just an inch away from his face, printing only in the precise spots and by-passing the rest. It's like being inside a printer! It would print on him as easily.

The spin and the whirr of each pass makes him imagine different faces. Nicole, as she struggled with Khurana in the park; Zameer, as his back arched; Rossane, whom he must find; Khurana's killer baying silently at the sky after the kill…her silhouette a perfect match with the image of the Garou that the Dai-Osho drew; the shadows that Tashi created in the library; maid; pugs… Flashes of incomplete faces; a printer is printing on a woman's face; Nicole, as she laughed and chatted the night Khurana died; Nicole, as she looked at her digital facial reconstruction; Rumana, as she clawed at him across the table in the police station…

The clerk comes back and peeps under the grid.

'Nothing in our data, but then there are some artists who give themselves names. This guy here calls himself the flaming sun and last month, we had a songbird…'

The artist realizes that artistic appreciation is not Vikram's aim at all. He gets irritated and demands Vikram come out immediately.

'Hey, what do you think you are doing? Security… Security…' the artist calls out. Vikram surfaces from under the structure. He gives the half-formed faces one last look. Leaves.

36

Mindfuck

Vikram is in Raghav's office.

'You've hit five million,' Raghav informs him.

Vikram smirks, 'Cool. And you?'

Raghav just gives him a cold stare. The two men continue to eye ball each other for a few moments. In a crazy twisted sort of way, the rating on the betting site created by the killer has become a personal thing for the two of them. Raghav is not happy about being the less 'hot' item.

Tashi watches the two of them, not as the junior-most officer in the room but as a woman observing two idiotic men. Having had enough, she places her file on the table with a deliberate sharp sound. Raghav sees it and slides it towards Vikram.

'Smith sent it, they cracked one payment gateway on the betting site which had Khurana on it.'

Vikram opens the envelope.

'It has a list of five receiving bank accounts spread across the globe. Unfortunately, the link between this betting website that collected money and her website that screened Khurana's killing doesn't exist,' says Raghav.

'There is no way we can prove that this money was paid for this killing. No way to get an official demand for those banks to co-operate...and unless we can do that, this is only information, not evidence,' Tashi adds.

'The bank accounts will probably be empty by now. She will

have converted everything into hard cash and stashed it away as gold, diamonds and stuff,' concludes Vikram.

Raghav has more news, 'Now that we have the DNA match we are officially registering Zameers's homicide.'

'But we are nowhere near getting Rossane, it could very well drive her away,' Vikram argues.

He notices Raghav's eyes darting towards his laptop screen. It seems to be happening involuntarily, even when his body is slightly turned away. Then in the smoky glass pane behind Raghav's chair, he sees a reflection. Raghav's eyes have been darting towards the screensaver.

The screensaver is a single erotic frame from Zameer's killing. The killer astride Zameer, head thrown back.

The intensity of her influence once again dawns on Vikram. A complete mindfuck, a complete suspension of rationale even amongst the most hardened. That's what she had managed to achieve, her act was calling out in a manner more primal than the sex. It was a duel, a challenge. Every man who saw her wanted her, knowing fully well she fucked to kill. Perhaps, every man was an ass who believed he would better her.

If she comes for Raghav, he was a goner for sure. But she wouldn't come for Raghav, she would come for him, Vikram. Was he really all that different than Raghav?

'If only Rossane comes online again…' Raghav sighs.

Tashi is surprised, 'You want her to kill again?'

'You do remember one of us has to be the next target?' Vikram smirks.

Raghav shrugs, 'Our friend Smith has promised to tag it instantly, Shekhar and team have been authorized access to trace the website.'

They watch, bemused, as Raghav speaks to the killer's image

on his laptop, 'Come on, Rossane... one more time...'

Tashi and Vikram leave the room, out in the corridor.

'And what if she doesn't come online again?' Tashi wonders.

'Do you want her to?'

They both smile and turn towards Raghav's office.

'Now, that would be a really ugly sight...' Tashi grimaces.

37

@Kong

Vikram's office, @kong enters, stands in front of Vikram, shifting his weight from one leg to another.

'What?' Vikram finally acknowledges his existence.

@kong places a dozen pictures in front of Vikram. They are pictures of Nicole in half a dozen different refugee camps across Europe and Africa. 'She volunteered, with different UN groups…three to four-month stints in each place. Mosul in Iraq, the jungle in Calais, Munigi base in Congo, Moria in Greece… found these in the official records…face recognition software… restricted authorization…'

Vikram is studying the photos and barely aware of @kong droning away in the background.

'Please, Sir, I don't want to get into trouble…. It's…'

The word *trouble* gets Vikram's attention, 'What trouble?'

'These were not in the public domain, some UN agencies keep the identities of their workers confidential.'

'So, basically, you hacked into some HR site.'

'Something like that. Sometimes folks in the psychiatric section end up knowing stuff, so to protect…'

Vikram has tuned off again.

All the pictures had been taken when she was unaware, at work. Like informative pictures taken for official record. In sanitized interiors, in overcrowded camps, in the squalor outside the camps, in the bombed-out rubble…

What was she doing there? Why had she gone there? Was she a violence groupie? Seeking violence and strife, seeking human anguish, seeking blood and gore, wanting to look into the eyes of killers…. Shit! What was wrong with him, it was he who was obsessed with looking into the eyes of the killer. Her presence in all those places had a justification, they were her natural domain. Post-trauma criminal psychology. There couldn't be a better place to practice it.

Vikram once again becomes aware of @kong standing there, shifting from foot to foot.

'What? Ya…ok. Good work. Look for Rossane, everywhere. My responsibility. Whatever you find, bring it straight to me.'

@kong charges out, enthusiastically. He had been authorized to look 'everywhere'. For a moment, Vikram envies the child in that man. Lucky guy, life hasn't sullied him completely as yet.

It doesn't seem to have sullied Nicole either, if she can still go back to these hives of death and misery and actually hope to make a difference. Vidya was like that, a perpetual optimist.

Vikram is not like that. He believed in humanity's ability to fuck itself and everything it touched. It was going to implode before the end of the next millennium and nature was going to reclaim everything, just like in Chernobyl…and the wolves would take over. Why the fuck was he mulling on Chernobyl and wolves when there was so much to be done.

The Garou…the wolf-like Garou…the bracelet! The bracelet that the killer wore, with the exquisite beast faces and the diamond fangs that she used on her victims. That's where he had seen the Garou. That's why it looked familiar when the Dai-Osho drew it. Vikram felt a momentary satisfaction of being on the right track. But how long would his wait last…?

Rossane, Rossane, Rossane, don't you want to collect your millions? Why haven't you reached me?

He locks the office door. Opens the window, shoos off some sleeping pigeons. They flutter blindly in the darkness. He knew what that felt like, he had been fluttering in the darkness too. He perches on the eight-inch ledge. Legs dangling over the fifteen-storey drop to the road below. He pulls out the marijuana packet concealed in the undercarriage of the air-conditioning duct. This is what Tashi had been searching for unsuccessfully in his office.

He rolls a joint. He had been doing this for the past two years, since moving into this office.

The sea wind carried the smoke and scents away. The street lights never reached so high up and left him in darkness. He had always enjoyed these moments. It gave him an extra kick to be smoking the marijuana here, just two floors above the narcotics department's office.

A long deep drag…exhale…repeat…repeat…it did nothing for him, nothing at all. That's how it had been since he killed Vidya. Killed Vidya, that's how he always worded it. Somehow, calling it her death, distanced him from it, from her. He did not want that distance.

But the edgy dull throb inside him was not about Vidya. It was about the yearning to look into the eyes that Zameer had looked into. Why the fuck was he wasting time…? Why was he waiting till she reached him? And he had no doubt she would. If not the money, the challenge would bring her forth. He crushes the joint against the wall and flings it away. Before it hits the ground, he has shut the window and is on the move.

To start at the beginning is the only way…

38

The Beginning

Vikram reaches Nicole's home. She is on her terrace, reading. The pugs greet him at the door excitedly and start their routine welcome: barking, jumping, snapping, humping. Vikram is cursing and hopping around as he tries to shake them off. Nisha gives Vikram a funny look, then recognizes him.

'Waterproofing?' she wants to know.

Vikram sighs, so much for his elaborate moustache. 'Not this time. Take them away…'

Nisha is unsure and suspicious.

Nicole appears, 'It's ok…'

Nisha tries to grab the pugs, they run around the room making her chase them. She manages to grab them and still struggling, locks them in the bedroom. Vikram watches her go. Silence at last. 'This would be a good time to go into hiding for a bit,' he tells Nicole.

She is taken aback. Vikram picks up the wire she uses for her bonsai and tries bending it absent-mindedly. It's tougher than he had anticipated. 'She is more vulnerable than you, we know she is one of your patients, not maid,' indicating towards Nisha. He manages to bend the wire. 'Rossane's DNA matched the hair at Zameer Khan's murder location.'

'Rossane! Oh… Wow…that's…well, I would have never thought she could…but then, I didn't really have her for long.'

'You are the one who picked her from the whole lot. So, there must have been a reason.'

'This is…very disturbing.'

Vikram continues working on the wire, bending it one way, then the other way.

Nicole asks, 'So now, what happens?'

'We find her and bring her in.'

'That's a relief, I…'

'First, we need to find her.' Vikram's eyes are boring into her.

'What? I don't know…'

'Come on! You pulled her from over a thousand patients. Something rang a bell, something inside you knows.'

Nicole is silent, his logic is irrefutable. The dogs are unhappy being locked and start whining in the bedroom. The sound grates on Vikram's nerves. 'We need to unravel this from the beginning. I need you to come with me,' he tells her.

'Where?'

'Mount Kilauea.'

Nicole looks clueless.

'That's where she trained. Shiro the Garou master…'

'Shiro the what? I don't know what you are talking about. She never mentioned anyone by that name.'

Vikram shrugs.

'Let me get this straight. You warned me I could be watched. Then you land up at my home late at night. You tell me Nisha and I could be in mortal danger. Then you ask me to go with you to the other side of the world to find a woman I haven't seen for years and some Shiro master I have never heard of. Why would I do that?' Nicole is clearly alarmed.

Vikram is searching for the right words. The pugs' protest session is gaining momentum. One lets out a long painful howl. Just as it is losing steam, the other takes over. Damn the dogs. It is unnerving and interrupting his thought process. He knows she is a whisker away from refusing and he can't allow her to do that.

'It's her hair versus your face.' It has come out all wrong, but that's what it basically is.

Nicole has a strange look of bewilderment on her face. Vikram digs in harder.

'Her hair on the beach with Zameer can be dismissed as circumstantial evidence. Your face...on the woman riding him to death—that can be declared conclusive evidence.'

'Are you crazy? It wasn't me. You know it, I...'

Vikram digs his heels in, 'They will officially announce Zameer's murder any minute now. I will need to act. That's how it will go. She is missing, you are here. I know it couldn't have been you...but I would have to arrest you. So help me find her. Now.'

Vikram is watching her closely. A silence descends on her. He is trying to block out the high pitch of the dogs, a numb ache has started at the back of his head. *Focus...focus on her*, his mind is demanding. *Be prepared to counter any resistance, you need this.* After one whole minute, she nods.

'We leave now,' he tells her.

39

Silence

At Mumbai airport, a decidedly nervous Nisha is sent off on a flight to Bhubaneswar with instruction to lie low till she hears from Nicole. She holds on to Nicole's hand till the very last moment, Nicole whispers to her reassuringly. Watching from afar, Vikram notices the subtle body changes in Nisha as Nicole prepares her for the moment of parting. Nisha blinks back tears when she has to finally turn away.

She never looks back. Just walks away. It is Nicole who watches her for a long time before turning away. Vikram is intrigued.

A man approaches Vikram, hands over a non-descript brown bag. It contains his and Nicole's passport with a US visa stamp. Courtesy of Mr Smith.

His mobile rings. It is Smith. 'You get me the team that designed CMND-Z blocked. The killer is yours.'

Whatever or whoever it was that employed Smith, if that really is his name, had judged Vikram suitable to be used as a foot soldier. Their interest lay in acquiring and controlling each innovation that had the power of disruption.

Of humans, by humans, for humans. That's what data was all about. And the no man's land they operated in, sought out men like Vikram, who are ready to work for self-interest beyond the law.

Smith didn't care if the murders were solved, if the killer was apprehended. He wanted to reach the systems she had created to operate and disappear with such impunity. It would, of course, be preferable if the killer was neutralized rather than standing trial in India and having her modus operandi revealed. The gun Vikram had asked for would be given to him once they landed. As for Vikram's payoff, he was bidding his time. What Smith wanted… he was welcome to want. What Vikram wanted…he didn't know, as yet.

Nicole and Vikram board the flight and settle down in their seats. The next twenty hours, Nicole spends in silence. Every effort to draw her into a conversation is met with polite silence. And then she falls asleep.

Vikram studies her from the corner of his eye. Not wanting to stare directly. The harsh reading light above his seat lights her face partially. Her sleeping face is calm and balanced. If he had hoped that she would sleep-talk…that wasn't happening. He realizes staring is going to get him nowhere. Gives up. Switches off the light, settles down to rest.

He is not looking forward to searching in the great outdoors, the wide open skies. Vidya would have loved it. It was finally the wide open skies that betrayed her.

The wind is like a whiplash when you open the aircraft door at seven thousand feet. And then she jumped. With her flying suit and a go-pro strapped to her forehead. Everything had gone as planned. She hit the safety net with precision. Then got thrown up again by the momentum. When she landed back into the net, she was a crumpled doll. Somewhere in the last six seconds when she was thrown back into the air, her spinal cord had snapped. A freak accident. By the time she was in the hospital, she had slipped into a coma she never woke up from.

Vikram is gripped by the intense shock of that long-ago moment. He knows he is going to need the rest of the flight to rid his body of the chemical cocktail that the extreme emotion has created. He can't afford to focus on anything but the killer right now.

A few hours later, exhausted by his internal conflict, he falls asleep.

40

Kīlauea

Hawaii, Base of Mount Kīlauea.

Vikram has serious doubts about his plan by the time they find themselves at the base of Mount Kīlauea. It towers over them in the distance, clouds of grey gas and vapour cover the lava lake high above. The occasional ash rising from the mouth and the sizzling of the lava hitting the water are a constant reminder, the volcano is alive and waiting. Their guide draws them away from the crowd of tourist milling around and posing on the solidified lava flows.

They walk past signs with 'Danger', 'Stop'.

'…the last volcanic explosion…my village barely escaped. Officially, we are not permitted to go beyond this point,' the guide is telling them.

The ravages of the eruption are everywhere. The eerie patterns of the hardened flow of lava are fascinating. It seems as though the stone is alive and resting, any moment, it will flow again. They walk over lava flows, then hit small clearings of green, then back on to the lava flows. They have been walking for two hours now, there is no other tourist in sight. The guide had taken Vikram's demand seriously when he had said: 'Take us where we won't see a single soul around.'

'Sure my friend, just remember that the soul of Kīlauea can never be left behind as long as you tread on its territory.' The guide had said dramatically while leading them away.

Super clichéd though it sounded, here in the land of exploding earth, Vikram is ready to give it some credit. The guide keeps on a constant flow of touristy information, 'This pattern of the lava is called the elephant's hide, and then there is pahoehoe, it looks like a rope…now a'a is very different from…'

Vikram is drinking in the environment. The cloak of silence that had descended over Nicole is palpable to even the guide and all his conversation is addressed only to Vikram.

Vikram is not here to study the lava. It's Shiro he is after. 'Shiro you say?' the guide quickly grabs this new angle. 'Not many outside my village could have heard of him. You are lucky you found me…'

He takes a marked turn to the right and starts down an invisible trail. Pointing halfway up a slope that is now covered with hardened lava, 'Shiro lived somewhere up there. Lots of natural caves. Very dangerous.'

'Isn't it prohibited by the government?' Vikram asks.

'But who was going to tell him that? He never came into town. Nobody's seen him since the eruption. Earlier, the pilots flying tourists over the mountain would catch a glimpse of him… sometimes…'

Nicole has pulled out a pair of binoculars and is scanning the slopes.

Vikram mulls over what the guide told them, 'So he could be dead?' The guide opens his arms in a dramatic gesture, 'The mountain swallows without leaving a trace.'

'… or he could be alive?'

The guide realizes that this man would rather believe that Shiro was alive, so decides to flow with it. What the hell, if it will get him a bigger tip! 'Yes, yes, he could be. Three men from my village, given up for dead, walked down from the mountain five days after the explosion. The Goddess Pele had chosen to spare them.'

Vikram is a bit reassured, 'Did people come to see him?'

'There were some who would come seeking him and ask for directions in the local pub. When they left...if they leave...no one knows.'

'Why do you say that?' Vikram asks.

They have walked around a sharp bend on the slope. He is looking seawards. The guide is distracted. He would have loved to give this man a big speel on Shiro, but there was a more urgent worry heading his way right now. The guide once again dramatically throws his arms open, 'Look, it is coming. You guys are lucky, this happens just a couple of times in a year.'

A cloudbank moves rapidly towards them. It's a mesmerizing sight. 'What is happening?' Vikram asks. 'Stop!' the guide commands. 'Do not move an inch. Low rain clouds, ash and gases from the volcano create a whiteout...'

Within moments they are completely covered. Vikram holds his hand in front of his eyes. Can't see anything. It's a whiteout. He can feel the smell of trapped sulphur fumes burn the edge of his nostrils. The scent of the volcano. That's what it is, he feels his skin tingle. He is breathing in the depths of the earth.

Vikram talks into the white nothingness, 'This makes us lucky! How long does it last?'

'Madam, stay where you are, don't move,' the guide calls out in the nothingness. No response, but considering Nicole's suborn silence; that would be her only response.

Knowing nature cannot be hurried, the guide squats on the ground and starts whistling a local song, perfectly comfortable in the nothingness. Vikram is getting edgy by the moment. Blind with eyes wide open, it's not for him. Claustrophobia in the white void is gripping him tighter and tighter. It's barely ninety seconds, yet it feels like several minutes to him. This was a crazy unknown world and it is unnerving him.

Involuntarily, he turns around and takes a step, immediately stumbles.

Just before the whiteout, Vikram had lost sight of Nicole who was trailing behind. He really should check on her. He pulls out a pair of goggles from his small backpack. Presses a button, the lens converts into a thermal imaging glass. The warm ground shows up. It is of a higher temperature than the cool cloudbank. No sign of a human figure. He would have sworn she was right behind them. He starts moving cautiously in the direction where Nicole should be. He struggles and slips but keeps moving. The whistling of the guide is getting softer and softer as he moves away from him.

He is scanning from left to right, to left...

Then a figure moves into his field of vision. A figure moving precisely and effortlessly through the blind treacherous terrain. Vikram freezes.

The whiteout has made no difference to this person. Moving higher and higher, the person almost passes him...then stops and faces him squarely. Eyeballing him, if such a thing is possible in a whiteout!

The hair on Vikram's nape stands up. He can feel the laser-sharp intensity of the person's vision hit him. Vision? How the hell can there be any vision in this whiteness? Unless of course, the other person was also wearing thermal vision googles like him.

For a moment, Vikram feels silly for having been unnerved.

41

Hold the Gaze

The mist clears, almost like a veil lifting to reveal a secret. Vikram finds himself looking into the eyes of the killer. In an instant the picture is complete. That which Vikram saw, lying on the sand, impersonating Zameer in his death, the killer rising above him, looking down at him...her gaze, steady, hooded, mesmerizing... drawing in death...

Nicole has locked eyes with him. Her entire persona has transformed. From the benign woman to an alpha killer. She has chosen to reveal herself.

As Vikram recognizes her for what she truly is, the bile rises inside him. In that fraction of a moment, which seems to extend for so long, Vikram comes to a decision. Just as the panic is hitting his eyes, a smile lights up his face. Almost like having finally met a long lost friend. Everything his unconscious had registered, everything his heart had recognized, stands true in front of him.

He is looking into the face he was searching for. It was not the assembly of eyes, nose mouth...it was the gaze of the apex predator...

Of all the responses, this is not what Nicole expected.

'It's time to head back,' the guide calls out.

Vikram knows this is the point of no return.

CMNDZ–blocked.

No retrieve, no undo, no undelete... This was a one-way street... He readies himself for it.

She watches him, supremely alert. Perched on the rock, framed against the volcano, she emits an eerie power.

Vikram pays the guide and adds a hefty tip. The guide, his conscience suitably satisfied, leaves the two in the treacherous landscape and heads back to bait the next tourist. Vikram turns and looks up at her, it's a look bordering on reverence. He raises his hand to his head, eyes twinkling, he snaps into a full-blown military salute.

'Respect!'

Nicole appears unmoved, superbly concealing the surprise that his action must have evoked in her. Vikram is acutely aware of her studying his slightest movement. She is micro mapping Vikram's body language, the rise and fall of his chest as he breathes, counting his rate of breathing, figuring his heart rate and anxiety status. His over-steady unblinking gaze. The position of his legs and arms, studying his body contour, searching for hidden weapons.

She registers the small bump on his ankle where the handgun is strapped.

Vikram is acutely aware of the danger. He has to be super calm. He has to go all the way, there are no half measures with this woman. He puts his hands up in the air as though she were holding a gun to him. It's a strange sight; an unarmed woman, by sheer force of her persona, makes an armed man give up his weapon.

Making his intentions very clear, Vikram slowly reaches for where the gun is concealed and slips it out. Click. He removes the magazine. Lets it slip to the ground.

'You can kill me any moment with your bare hands…we both know it… I am putting my life in your hands…knowing that it will be safe… I want you to trust me…'

He has his hands in the air, he rotates so that she can see him from all angles. Her eyes are inscrutable.

Vikram continues with disarming humility, 'The world is a big place, and the true student will come drawn to the true master. That's what Sensei Shiro believed…isn't it.'

There is just a flicker of a long-forgotten emotion on Nicole's face. Vikram instantly responds to it

'You never sought him yet you reached him. I too never sought you, yet I reached you… For the very reason that you loved him, respected him so deeply…and have become his truest student… I fell in love with you, grew to respect you and came here in search of you… The spirit of the Garou can never be taught, we have to be born with it. To kill is an honour, I want to earn it!'

His face glows with a genuine earnestness…because he is speaking the truth, finally the truth.

The weight of much deceit lies heavy on him. Sure, he had admitted to having killed the rapist Sunny but he had not pulled the trigger; it had been the victim's teenaged son. He had driven the young boy's rage, compelled him to kill. Vikram's job had provided him with the cloak of safety, he had used it to protect the kid and send him off… or so he told himself.

He had never fired the gun, snapped the neck, run a truck over the trapped body… He had gotten others to do it for him.

A family member, a friend, a lover…violent deaths created volcanoes in the hearts of the survivors. Over the years, through trial and error, he had learnt to convert the rage, anguish and bloodlust of another person into a weapon. A weapon he wielded masterfully; achieving the death of his chosen villain in the manner that suited him.

And so, Sunny the rapist had been shot…

The drunken driver who ran over the family on the overloaded scooter…had been crushed under the truck tyres driven by a brother... The woman who drove her father-in-law to commit suicide had been forced to jump off a stool and be hung to death by a broken husband... Six in ten years... Had he not chosen their death, all of them would have been alive. Had he not chosen, their killers would not have killed.

He had recognized in her face an apex predator, a master, a warrior. Something that he ached to be... It made him shamefully aware that he was just a ham-handed serial fucking motivator of killers... It sounded so lame but there, he had admitted it! He was nothing but a mere bumbling opportunistic arsehole. Too weak, too afraid to get the blood on his hands. All the righteous venom he had wiped up inside himself each time before the kill...it was just play-acting...meaningless justification.

Watching Nicole kill had opened up a gate inside him.

... And he had killed for the first time, with his own two hands. Pulling the plug on his Vidya was his first direct kill. To take life was an honour. He was painfully aware that he had not earned it.

That's why he wanted to reach her. He wanted to be her. The Dai–Osho had seen the hunger in him, so had Smith. That was the only payoff he had sought.

Choosing to take a life and carrying it through, creates a sensibility and awareness that others can never intuit. Across the world, every race forced young fighters to kill as a passage to manhood, to become soldiers, warriors...predators.

That's why he stood there unarmed, vulnerable and deeply in love with this creature. He is looking into the eyes of a person from another time and sensibility. Just a century ago, her skills would have been respected. She wouldn't be hiding, only hunting.

42

Rossane

Late into the night, nearly dawn.

Mumbai.

@kong peeps into Vikram's office for the tenth time. Not finding Vikram in, he stands there shifting his weight from one leg to another, staring into space. He is carrying a bunch of pictures.

In her search for Rossane, Tashi is scanning through the data flowing in from the US. No luck. Nothing at all. Sleep-deprived and over-worked, she is annoyed at Vikram. He is gone again, mobile phone conveniently switched off. Leaving her alone to tackle the search for Rossane and the increasingly impatient Raghav.

The newly placed TV is running silently on the wall in front of her. Raghav and the powers that be had decided twelve hours ago that it was time to acknowledge Zameer's death. Of course, the snuff video had not been mentioned. The news had simply swept everything aside on the national front. Loud opinionated busybodies, anchors and experts were screeching from every channel.

All their speculation was so tame against the reality. Had she not been so exhausted, Tashi would have had a good laugh. To keep searching was all she could do. If only @kong would stop shuffling his feet and hanging around outside Vikram's door like a puppy.

'What?' she snaps.

@kong is not sure if he should respond. He decides not to, starts to walk out.

'What?' she asks him again.

'Nothing, Vikram Sir had asked me to look up Rossane...'

'Buddy, that's what we are all doing, what's that in your hand?' She has pried it out of his hands even before he can stop her. Three pictures of Rossane. The first, posing, wearing a headscarf and holding a Kalashnikov-type assault rifle. 'What the hell is this?'

@kong mumbles some explanation, 'I don't know if it's her...'

Tashi is studying the picture closely, the face is much leaner, much harder, the headscarf has covered her cheeks partially, 'It is her, where is this...'

'We were searching in the US, wrong place. This is Mosul, Iraq.'

'ISIS?'

'No, no...rebel group...some kind of offshoot...too damn confusing.'

Tashi is looking at the next picture. She is in military fatigues. No scarf, the hair is tied in a top knot, the hair dye is striking. It's the same as the sample given by Nicole.

'Oh shit!' she curses.

She is now looking at the last picture. It's a picture taken almost like a mugshot, only the person is lying on the ground and is dead. A dead body with a partially disfigured face. What remains of it looks alarmingly like Rossane. The same low hairline, receding chin. But the nose was completely gone, so was the entire left side of the face.

@Kong says, 'From the gallery of the unknown dead. Photos of unidentified dead bodies across Syria, Yemen, Iraq, are uploaded there. For families to search...'

Tashi sits down on her chair. This is bad news. The dead body, it was damn close, but was it really her?

@Kong reads her mind, 'It was taken nearly a year ago. The

facial match was sixty per cent. So, it is totally possible that it's not her.'

Tashi covers the disfigured part of the face with her hand and peers closely, 'To be expected, there is only half a face to recognize... It is also quite possible that it is her. Keep searching, it's critical.'

Tashi knows that if this is for real, it changes everything. But the DNA match with the hair on the beach? And that damn hair colour...! Was there an explanation? Or would it mean pressing 'Restart' again? This is going to make Raghav mad.

43

Rising Demons

Kilauea.

They have been walking for over half an hour. Nicole ahead, uncaring that Vikram is following behind, out of her line of sight. That unsettles Vikram. Is it an act of trust or disdain? He prays it's the former. His brain is awash with unexperienced emotions.

Vikram speaks, a tinge of quiver occasionally creeping into his voice, 'The evidence is piling up, it is just a matter of time. I wanted to reach her…you…for myself. To make sure you remained free. Free to be yourself…everything about you is perfect, just the way it should be! The world will never accept your strength… You have to be protected.'

Protected? The irony in his passionate statement surprises her. It is probably he who needs protection…from her! She chooses to remain silent. Knowing her silence will prod him to keep talking, while she takes stock of the situation and him.

Vikram keeps talking, 'In discovering you, I discovered myself… Your energy, your ability and the sheer beauty…unlocked me… Gave me a goal.'

A dam has burst inside Vikram, he cannot stop the flow of words. He dare not stop.

Because, in recognizing her, he had recognized himself. Because, only the clamour of his voice can push back the self-knowledge he has arrived at.

Pulling Vidya off the life support had changed him forever.

The slow stopping of her breath, the final sigh. His broken sob, silenced violently. He had not been able to keep her safe from death, to protect her... Yet, her death had been a release.

As her body went still, his tortured face had dropped its weight momentarily, relief and energy flashing through. Then the wave of loathing, at himself for having felt that way, had overtaken him. And now...here it had morphed itself into raging energy to rise, to live...unrepentant.

Vikram needs the words, 'I cannot, will not allow you to be hunted...caged...killed this time, I will not fail.'

Nicole sees the demons inside him rising and falling. Strangely, it makes her calmer. Demons, she understands. 'What was your sister to you?' she asks softly.

Vikram freezes. She had read his mind! How did she know? How much about his life does she know? Truth is the only way forward. 'Everything. She was the keeper of my conscience. Killing her was the most difficult act of my life.'

'Yet you could do it.'

44

Overmatched

Mumbai. Raghav's office.

Tashi and Malhotra wait for Raghav to digest their latest news. The dead woman in the picture was Rossane. Raghav looks like he is already imploding. 'If she died in Mosul a year ago, then what was her hair doing on the beach? How did the damn DNA match?'

Tashi reads out the DNA report matching Rossane's hair to the hair found on the beach.

'It says a hundred per cent match. Samples identical in all parameters. Identical. Both hairs are the same. That's what it meant.'

On her laptop, she has images of the two hair once again.

She continues, 'Look at the area of the blue-green dye from Nicole's sample. Now, look at the one we collected on the beach. It is identical. The hair we found on the beach was recoloured burgundy over the earlier blue-green dye. So, essentially, when the lab declared a match it was not just for the DNA, but the complete hair!'

'So, it could have been recoloured hair from the batch Nicole gave you?' Raghav asks.

Tashi nods.

'Arrest Nicole!'

'For what? She has an impeccable alibi for each killing. Plus, she is gone. Three days ago. Vikram personally told her to go into hiding, till we had a grip over the Rossane situation.'

Raghav seems to sink deeper. They did not have enough to arrest Nicole. A Portuguese citizen, arresting her would set off many things. Arresting, and then having to release her again would make him look really bad.

Then a strange gleam starts building in his eyes, maybe there was still hope. Maybe Vikram had not taken off on one of his usual spells... Maybe, this time, it was different...

Tashi outthinks him, 'No. I don't think the killer has got to Vikram, if she had, by now his video would have been up.'

45

To See You

Kilauea.

Nicole has destabilized Vikram completely, her inscrutable eyes boring into him, reading god knows what! Vikram struggles to get back in control. This woman is fire, the only way to do it is to shift the focus back to her.

'No matter how many faces you juggled, how many alibis and fake leads you threw my way, no matter what the DNA reports say… I kept coming back to this…' He is holding out the digital image he created of her. 'Perhaps that is why I felt the need to bring you here…'

Nicole turns away and starts walking upwards. He follows, struggling a bit to keep pace, to talk to her face, not her back. Where the fuck is she going…what is he walking into? There is a tight knot in Vikram's stomach. *Keep talking. Keep talking.* He tells himself.

'You used the 3D digital printer to create the different faces, right? The beach boys saw you with Rumana's face that morning. You did that to put Rumana on the spot. But Zameer wouldn't have had anything to do with her after the trouble on the set, and anyway, you had no plans of letting your face be seen in the film. So you choose to kill him as yourself.

On your return journey, when the fishing trawler crew saw you, you were Rumana again. Such a fucking simple old-fashioned trick and it would have worked. Your face in Zameer's eyes was a one in a million chance, but it happened, and I saw it. I found you. It was our destiny!'

Vikram's face reflects an overwhelming conviction. Destiny. That is the one undeniable fact that had brought him here.

'All your alibis…it was Nisha pretending to be you. It was her walking the dogs in the park on the day Zameer was killed and on the day Suraj was killed… It threw us off the track. Then I saw her chasing the pugs, she would get breathless so easily, the body language, it said something to me… You sedated Tashi that night. Then put on Tashi's face and killed Khurana.'

'He was a fool.'

Her response sends a chill through Vikram's bones. It is an admission of all her actions. It is an acceptance of everything he had inferred about her so far. It calls for a celebration. Vikram, the standup comic, comes to the surface. He laughs and jiggles his butt the way Khurana had done in the film. He looks worse than Khurana had. Nicole unconsciously relaxes, half smiles.

'But why him?'

'What he did to Nisha was unpardonable.'

Nicole had returned home early that morning and found Nisha curled up on the floor, whimpering, like a broken doll. Nicole, who had just killed a brute of a man, tenderly held her and rocked her for a long time. She noticed the nail marks on her arm and bruises on her chest and shoulder. She patiently coaxed Nisha to draw the image of her attacker.

'He had to go,' says Nicole.

Vikram, still unsure about how to handle her responses, blurts out, 'But then you found out that I had given the order, so why not me?'

'Are you trying to convince me that I killed the wrong guy?'

Vikram feels a sudden chill, 'Fuck! No! Not at all... I mean... I understand. You needed an alibi for that evening, so she had to go to the park. She is super fragile, that's why I insisted you send her away before we came here.'

She holds up her hand, indicating that Vikram should stop his nervous rambling. Vikram realizes that they are standing at a place of significance.

They are at the edge of a large field of solidified lava.

'This is where I first met Shiro.'

46

Student

Fifteen years ago.

A teenaged Nicole is resting against a rock, pouring water over herself, from a bottle, to cool off. A long trek had brought her here. The 'Mission Hope' T-shirt is soaked with sweat, the high humidity in the atmosphere has her hair clinging to her scalp. The solo trek every weekend was her time away from the charity hospital she was volunteering at for the summer.

The ground is covered with ferns, the eruption has not engulfed the land as yet. She senses a movement in the undergrowth. Looks around, nothing. Her presence probably disturbed some nesting birds. She feels the hair on her nape stand up, as though responding to an unseen presence. She turns around... Shiro.

What the fuck!

She sees nothing but his eyes. Dark slits with a mesmeric gaze. So important in a duel to earn that fraction of a moment that stands between life and death.

He looks her over, sneers.

He turns around and starts walking, briskly. She hesitates just for a moment, then follows him, can't keep up. Alarm bells are ringing loud in her head, voices are screaming at her. *What are you doing? Who the hell is this man? This is crazy... Stop.*

She is half running, half stumbling behind him. It's a desperate jog, it disorients her, makes her dizzy, but she keeps going, higher and higher. Hour after hour...

They finally reach the opening of a camouflaged dwelling. She falls to her knees, coughing and breathless. The sun has set a long time ago. It's dark. The sea mist is coming in fast. Within moments, she is covered in it and shivering. Yet the soft grey blanket is strangely comforting. She curls into a ball on the stubbly floor, passes out.

She doesn't resist, barely wakes up when she feels strong arms lift her and carry her gently into the shelter. It strikes a far off memory of the priest picking her up from her mother's grave and carrying her to safety.

Back to the present.

Nicole has a faraway look on her face, that world is gone. There is nothing but dark grey crinkled earth around them.

Vikram asks, 'The story you told me about your mother and yourself...was true?'

Nicole nods imperceptibly, 'I came here to get away.'

Back to the past

Shiro is standing on the edge of a sheer drop. Then his body moves as though propelled by the slight gusts of wind, it's a strange tai-chi.

The young lonely girl watches him, intently, her own body moving unconsciously. There is wisdom in her eyes, she knows she is in the presence of a master. An instinctive recognition that cancelled out her common sense and propelled her to follow him.

He teaches her methods to fine-tune each separate sense. He teaches her to hear, to see, to smell. He teaches her to use her skin. Even the soft brush of air tells you something. Sometimes you know before you hear or see...

She spends days and weeks blindfolded... with her ears blocked. Only her breath and skin soaking in the world around.

Struck by a panic attack every few minutes, it takes a whole week till she finds her balance and silence.

Shiro had said to her, 'Your feet will recognize the ground you walk on and take you home on a dark moonless night.'

He teaches her to tune in to the unbroken communication between her and her whole environment. In their home, atop this volatile volcano, that could be the difference between life and death.

'Every emotion comes with its own scent. Recognize every whiff that emanates from your opponent. Death comes with its own scents and colours. Deflect it, least it becomes your own.' Shiro had told her.

She has been woken up in the dead of the night. Shiro is bending over her, speaking softly. She smells the faintest whiff of… something. He points to the flame of their small fire, the colour constantly changing, as different gasses seep through the ground to feed it. Their cave is the opening of a long-ago lava tunnel and the earth is reclaiming it.

Within minutes they are out in the open air.

It's time to learn about the human body, blindfolded, she traces every bone, muscle, pressure point on his body and her own. Precision is the weapon, not just force.

Late night. They are in the city. He flits through the shadows of the sleeping streets. She follows behind, inept still at the art of concealment. The backdoor of a shed opens for them. The scent of dead decaying flesh makes her physically gag. It would take countless trips to the local mortuary before the gagging reflex disappeared. A year later, she didn't respond to the stink at all. Her instincts had totally overcome the fear the stink aroused.

Smelling death is completely different from touching it. She learns to touch and dissect the stray unclaimed body that can be made available for them by the keeper of the mortuary. A man who gazed at Shiro with fear and devotion. All he wanted was to be allowed to watch as Shiro taught Nicole.

As one year flows into another...and then another...she never questions, never doubts. She can't really discern at what point he taught her combat. It seems to have flowed out of their daily rituals of mind and body exercises.

47

Garou

Late one evening, Nicole is returning after her stalking exercise for the day. It was quite simple actually. She would choose a group of tourists and stalk them through the day, moving through the undergrowth. The challenge was in making sure they never knew of her presence and she would return each time with a harmless trophy. A scarf, a water bottle, a packet of chips…

The day's trophy packet of chips had been eaten. As she approached their latest concealed cave, she hears a sound…startling and unexpected. It is Shiro laughing. A burst of loud open-hearted laughter. She stands still, drinking it in. This was a man she had lived with for four whole years, yet she had never heard him laugh…and now…

He is not alone, she hears a howl of delight, rather a growl of delight. There is another man with him. Suddenly unsure, she reaches the cave. There is another man for sure. A Japanese, just like Shiro. He might as well have been a clone of Shiro except that he is taller and heavier.

Neither of them takes any notice of her. Their rapid-fire chatter is gibberish to her. She watches them in amazement. Shiro the child, Shiro the man… She sees it all flit across his face. Childhood friends, they had to be. The easy camaraderie, the obvious bond… it had to be. She falls asleep. The men talk late into the night.

Thak, thak, thak. She wakes up to the sound of hard hand hitting bone. Within a fraction, she is on her feet ready to fight.

Shiro and his friend are in the midst of a duel. Bare armed, they are evenly matched. It is evident that the friend is no less a master at his art. For it feels like an art, a dance... as they move around each other, strike and evade, outwit and undermine. Never out of breath, never hurried or careless.

At first, she is unsure of what she should do. Then she realizes, she must do nothing. Just being there, watching, was a life-lesson for her.

And so it goes on for several hours. Nicole realizes why it won't stop. It can't. It's a duel to the death.

Garou.

The laughter, the emotion, the camaraderie of a few hours ago had been overcome.

Thhaank. Crack. The friend lands a precise blow on Shiro's leg. Nicole's heart sinks. Is this the beginning of the end? She is surprised when Shiro not only remains on his feet but swings that very leg forward to bring the friend down.

It's a perfect Kīlauea sunset, flaming red to complement the flaming lava pouring into the sea a few hundred feet below the cliff they are on. And the flaming red of the blood streaks that cover both men. Both are injured badly, both are drawing on some impossible reservoir of willpower and training within them.

The duel continues. It's now nearly twelve hours since they began. Both are unable to get to their feet. Sometimes, several minutes go by as they pass in and out of the pain and exhaustion-induced haze.

It finally ends fourteen hours after it started. When Shiro recovers from a nearly unconscious state just seconds before his friend. With a final burst of willpower, he crawls over, lifts himself and elbow facing down, drops on to his friend's neck.

Kaatacrrk! The spinal cord cracks. Shiro collapses over the body. It's over.

As Nicole tip-toes around them, she realizes Shiro has passed out again. He is still as death.

Its several hours before Shiro can sit up. With great difficulty, he kneels next to his dead friend and closes his eyelids. Shiro's face reveals neither remorse nor relief.

Then he starts digging, alone. Refusing to even acknowledge Nicole's presence. He buries his friend. Covers the grave. Kneels in prayer. As dawn rises, he opens his eyes and looks at her.

'You were afraid, of my death. That's not permitted. You have been trained to live like a warrior, now you must learn to die like one.'

A chill passes through Nicole's young soul. What does he mean? She is sure as hell not ready to die.

A whole month of careful nursing, under his precise guidance. Till Shiro is fully recovered. All thoughts of life and death have receded from Nicole's young eager mind. She is relieved to be getting back to their earlier routine.

Shiro informs her, 'Tomorrow, we will go into the city. Prepare yourself.'

48

Kill Street

Late night. Back alley of the town. She knows death is expected of her. She can feel the rising burn of acid inside her.

Shiro remains in the shadows, she walks out in the open.

He has chosen a place where she will be noticed and attacked.

It happens. As the man comes lunging at her, she gets five seconds, enough to map him. Five feet ten, between thirty-eight and forty years old, big built but no musculature, rotten teeth, the grip on the iron bar he intends to use on her is loose, the thumb of the right hand is jutting out as though with an old injury that has healed all wrong. His socks are a startling white, obviously stolen, he smells...of glue, sweat, tobacco and meat gravy...

She also maps herself, there is a light in her eyes, an excitement, a hunger. Her breath is even; skin, cool; eyes, sharply focused; muscles, alert yet unclenched... For the first time, she understands what Shiro saw in her... A natural warrior.

The fight is over in seconds. The attacker, a local low life thug, is no match for her, he is on the ground. The rod that was intended to land on her head is pressed down on his neck, just another ounce of pressure and his neck will cave.

More than the man at her mercy she is aware of Shiro's gaze... He is waiting...for her to land the fatal blow. The moment has arrived.

As she looks down at the frightened battered face cowering on the ground...she stops, she can't land the fatal blow, she was more than a match for him.

The victim sees her struggle with herself. He pushes away the rod from his neck, gets up and runs…she doesn't stop him…

Nicole is filled with an avalanche of emotions.

Shiro's soft voice comes out of the darkness, 'You did well. There is no honour in vanquishing a weakling. A warrior fights an equal…or more.'

Shiro wordlessly walks away. She trails behind him.

Another night, another place. This time the man is double her size, armed with a knife. He is more than her match. She fights him, gets hurled, punched and wounded. Till she turns the tables; a few sharp blows and to his complete shock, she has him pinned down.

In the heat and urgency of the moment, she raises her hands to bring them down into his jugular… This man she is supposed to kill. This is right. This is the 'moment' of her young life.

Like the talons of a raptor, her fingers shoot through the air at blinding speed…just millimetres away from his breathlessly throbbing throat…pulls back. An involuntary pull back.

Can't do it… Can't do it…can't kill him…

She has frozen.

A deep sense of humanity, an ingrained respect for life… She is faced with an invisible morality that she did not know existed inside her.

The man pushes her away and makes a dash for it, out of her reach.

Bruised, dishevelled and breathless, she remains kneeling on the wet miserable asphalt. Nicole doesn't have the nerve to get to her feet, to turn around, to face Shiro. She can feel his eyes burning into her back. She can feel his disappointment, rejection…

There is a deadly stillness, she suddenly swirls around. Something changed. He is no longer in the shadows, he is nowhere.

Garou—you either have it or you don't. She had let him down, he had abandoned her.

She stands at the base of the mountain. She can't get herself to climb up to him, she is no longer worthy of him, of his teaching.

She leaves, defeated, humiliated, heartbroken.

Back to the present.

She is standing there looking at the peak, her home, just as she had on that day long ago.

'I had let him down... I could never show him my face again...ever...'

Vikram's eyes are misted with tears that reflect her pain and loss. People go away from your life suddenly, irrevocably...he knows it well.

Nicole has never experienced this empathy, never allowed her true self to be seen by anyone other than her intended victim. She can't understand why she is sharing this with Vikram. This man, her hunter. Is it a weakness in her character, is she failing to hold the gaze of the adversary... Or is it that she is tired, so tired of the lonely life full of secrets. Coming back here has unsettled her, pulled down her defences, and she is feeling too drained to fight it.

With Vikram, she has unexpectedly given herself the luxury of truth and found a kindred spirit. A teardrop rolls down her cheek. She is once again the little girl who lost her world on her mother's death. This mountain is nothing but another painful grave that hid Shiro in its heart.

Instinctively, Vikram steps closer and encircles the little finger of her hand with his own. It's a gesture so close to the way he used to touch Vidya. A childlike act of connection and trust.

They stand there staring into the setting sun. It disappears once again when a dark cloudbank moves in, settling around them.

As the surroundings disappear, the pain attached to the place seems to evaporate a bit and Nicole speaks, 'I went back to studying. Working my way through college. I graduated. My break year. I was travelling with Ted, my boyfriend. Life was…so simple. My childhood, my times with Shiro… seemed to belong to another world…'

49
Sunshine

Nicole and Ted.

In the two months she had known him, she had laughed more than the rest of her young life put together. His easy charm and desire to live in the present was so refreshingly uncomplicated

Anoch Mor. Scotland.

A cosy log cabin hidden in the highlands. A dirt road leading up to it.

They rush in through the door, laughing and hugging. Completely disrobed even before they tumble on to the bed. The whole nature of this lovemaking is different, it's vibrant, playful, joyous…there is gentleness and comfort. The power play and dominance that had been ingrained into her by her years with Shiro is submerged. She has given herself the complete luxury of surrender. It has lulled her senses.

Somewhere his touch shifts gear, very subtly. The caress becomes playfully hurtful.

Next instant, Ted is riding her and choking her in the most crude and amateurish fashion. Involuntarily, her neck muscles have tightened into rock-hard cords.

She is looking at him with a strange deep sadness. He wants to kill her; for whatever reasons, he wants to kill her. This man is not a match to her in strength but his intention has betrayed her in a manner worse than her worst tormentor.

Time stretches as she does what she must… She effortlessly

slips back into her training.

Thaakh. In one continuous movement, she lifts her hips, dislodging him from her body. Her fingers yank at his thumbs, nearly tearing them off, into releasing her neck. Then propelling her body up, she swings over his flaying legs and lands on him.

Ted has never known or suspected this side of her and is stunned. There is raging anger in her when her fingers dive into his throat and pull out the jugular. She throws her head back in a scream as he dies. By instinct, she has performed her first ritual killing.

Why? Why?

She instinctively levels her breath. Emotion has played havoc with it.

As she gets off the bed she notices something. There is a large plastic sheet under the mattress. She starts pulling it out. Suddenly it dawns on her the sheet is there to contain the blood, the evidence, to wrap the body, her body. She realizes she is looking at something far bigger here. She washes the blood off and starts searching through the room.

Camera after camera. Ted was filming it all. He was going to film her killing. Film her killing! Why? What for?

Questions later. The same cameras now had footage of her killing him. She pulls out the chips.

She rolls his body up in the plastic neatly. Packs her stuff. She knows the place is awash with her fingerprints, there must be traces of the two of them everywhere. She is wondering about her next action.

She hears noises outside. It's a car. She rapidly climbs up and conceals herself amongst the rafters on the roof. Four men walk in. They have the keys to the main door. She remembers noticing them at the pub earlier in the day. They are calling out to Ted.

Two of them haul off Ted's body wrapped in plastic without even bothering to check it. They knew what would be in it. The whole thing was a setup. They had waited long enough to give him time to kill her.

They are going about it with a casualness that says they have done this before. One man is still calling out to Ted while the other starts opening the cameras to check the footage. He opens the first, nothing, then the second, nothing. Now he is edgy and she can isolate the tinge of panic in his voice, 'You need to see this…'

Up on the rafters, Nicole is like a deadly spider hovering over them, wondering if she should pounce, take them out. There's just two of them now, the other two are putting the body in the vehicle. She visualizes their killing. The leader is a fat pulpy middle-aged man, the other a flexed gym body, good for posing and nothing else. Yes, it can be done. Then decides to wait to learn more.

The leader takes a look into the camera. Finds nothing. He checks the other two. Nothing again. He rushes out. The plastic bundle has been loaded into the back of an SUV. They rapidly open it. There is silence and shock as they discover Ted's body instead of Nicole's.

To their experienced eyes, the method of killing is even more terrifying. It speaks of craziness and expertise that disturbs even their twisted minds.

She killed him. She outsmarted them. She could still be around. But they are four, she is alone.

The leader can almost feel her presence, he has nerves of steel, he barks an order. Clean the cottage. With a meticulousness that has come from practice, they return and clean the place.

Every surface is wet wiped. A heavy-duty vacuum cleaner picks every strand of hair that may have fallen on the floor, the rugs, on the furniture. The bathrooms are cleaned with bleach ensuring no body fluid shows up. Even the drains are pumped clean with bleach. Half-eaten food, contents of the refrigerator and garbage are collected and shrink wrapped for the incinerator. Ted's stuff is gathered and shrink wrapped for the incinerator.

Nicole watches as they erase every trace of her and Ted from the cottage. Her bag is left untouched. Then they get back into the vehicle and drive off.

Nicole gets down from her hiding place. She finds a slip of paper on the table, it looks as innocent as a family member leaving a note behind. The crafty leader has left an email address behind.

By cleaning up for her, he had made an offer.

50

Love

Back to the present.

'Once more a man had violated you. But he had also given you the opportunity of being worthy of Shiro!'

Nicole is a bit taken aback that Vikram has the same perspective as her. She says, 'With the footage from the cameras, I rushed back here... I wanted him to see, I wanted to see the pride in his eyes, only that would make me feel complete.'

Kīlauea.

Too late. There has been an eruption. Emergency services are carting out residents, villages have been emptied out. All approach paths to their earlier sites have lava flows moving forward relentlessly.

Everywhere, she is faced with the sizzling heat, the mesmerizing magma. Again and again, she encounters only firefighters and numbed homeowners. Some standing helplessly by and watching for hours as the magma eats into their homes.

She searches for him among the survivors, knowing fully well that he would never be there. She searches for him in every unaffected cave and shelter she can remember. Day after day, climbing, searching, making her way around treacherous flows.

He is not to be found. The mountain has claimed him.

She rages and rants at the mountain. She wanders, hidden from the world, living off the land as she had with him. The only man in her whole life, he gave her so much, made her everything she was, and she was not able to tell him that she had finally become worthy of him.

The loss is unbearable.

It is a loss she lives every waking moment, to this day.

Vikram faces Nicole squarely, 'I burnt every bridge before I made this journey with you. I will never leave your side…even though I fully know that you can…'

He mimics her hand blows on the bodies of the victims and the yanking of the jugular, then sticking his tongue out stupidly, he plays dead. He has instantly converted the brutality into a cartoonish act.

She is laughing, it is utterly funny. The ugliness of everything has been caricatured in a manner she never expected, and it's a relief. Her tensed body lets go, she gently leans against him. A subtle gesture, but for her a big act of trust.

'…no one will be surprised if I disappear, knowing that there is five million against my name on the portal…' Vikram assures her.

The last bit comes as a surprise to her.

'They know, they are doing their best to track it,' he adds. Thoughtful, Nicole leads the way to a small cave in the mountain.

'How many did you…?'

She simply smiles in return. Vikram whistles, impressed.

'And how much did you collect?'

'Twenty million, give or take a few…'

Vikram laughs, 'Whoa. There are really a lot of suckers out there!' The most lethal part of her being has been accepted so effortlessly. It can be so disarming.

'So how did you eat? You stalked, killed and prayed to the dead animal spirit, then cook and eat them?'

Nicole gives him a look that clearly says, 'Idiot!,' Out loud, she says,, 'This is not Avatar, buddy. Either Shiro or I went down in disguise to the supermarket and picked up rations.'

'Oh.'

Nicole throws him a slab of chocolate, 'This is a volcanic area, animals don't hang around here. At times, even birds keep clear of these skies.'

Vikram peels the wrapper, takes a bite into the slightly molten slab, the gooey chocolate makes conversation difficult for a few moments. It gives him time to think. Life is insane. He would never have imagined himself on that mountain slope sharing a slab of chocolate with the most impressive killer he had ever encountered.

But here he was, and it seemed so right. So far so good. She really was everything he had hoped for and more.

'It's just a matter of time before they reach Rossane, then?' he wants to know.

'She is dead.'

Vikram gets a start, 'Dead? You…'

Nicole's eyes go dark for a moment, he suspects her…after being told all this…

Vikram recovers rapidly, 'You wouldn't have harmed her, but she died, so you diverted the investigation towards her…'

'Something like that.'

'Now it makes sense…'

'What are you talking about?'

'The lab result on the hair. The matching DNA sent everyone on the chase. When the technician said the auburn hair and the sample hair you gave were identical, he meant it literally. You dyed it auburn and left it on the beach. On the off chance that it was discovered. And we discovered it.'

Nicole mocks him, 'You should have realized it earlier. Especially, after you realized the trouble I went through cleaning the sands. But you were too busy fantasizing.'

'There is much to learn. What did you plan to do with the money?'

Nicole laughs, 'I was wondering when you would come to that. Killing is expensive. Keeping secrets is expensive.'

'You made a great deal of it, much more than you needed for the secrets.'

'And then... then...there are my friends...like Nisha...they need to be protected until they find their strength again.'

This is the innermost part of Nicole. That which he would never have figured out by himself. She was choosing to disclose it. Vikram realizes she has been helping other women like her, using her money to keep them safe.

'How many did you...help? Where are they?'

Once again, Nicole merely smiles.

The sun is going down, it's becoming cooler. He is struggling to set up a fire. Nicole is watching him, he looks around for something to light. Opens his backpack. Removes some papers, tears the envelope and uses it to light the fire. He tosses the papers to Nicole.

'This is what they know. Why did you collect the money in banks? It makes you so vulnerable. Why not Bitcoins?'

Nicole scans the papers. The five accounts into which her money went are listed there.

She shrugs, 'Bitcoins couldn't have bought the things I needed, for myself and the others. Bitcoins don't buy your groceries, pay house rent, bus fare and school fees, lawyers' fees, security guards... They can look all they want, they will find nothing.'

'CMND–Z blocked, that's what Smith called it, it garbled

your websites beyond reach. Smith, the man who arranged our visas to get here.'

Vikram once again feels a silence descend on her. It's a silence that he cannot afford. Silence is mistrust, silence is separation. He can't bear to have a separation after having gotten so close...

He hurries on, 'He...they...whoever it is he represents... doesn't care about the killer getting caught or the money. He wants the systems that kept you safe. I am telling you this because you need to know the truth about everything. He, of course, thinks it is Rossane, and if he gets the info he wants, he will be off our back for good.'

Nicole is sinking deeper into her silence. Vikram continues, 'But the banks? They will hold the record of the transactions for good, then what? This can be eventually unravelled. By my team, by Raghav. What are we going to do then?'

Somewhere, he has shifted gear, he is now a co-conspirator, firmly by her side, pointing out loopholes, worrying.

'The money is out of the cycle already...at least out of their circle.'

Vikram emboldened, 'Don't be silly, there are ways...'

'It was physically withdrawn from each of these five accounts and the cash was deposited at completely different banks, different accounts. Some of it is already distributed, used...'

'As simple as that? No way, there could be records somewhere of the currency note numbers, trackers...it's just a matter of time...' Vikram is not convinced. Nicole smiles, 'Relax. It works. I've done it before.'

'No, no Nicole...they didn't know about the ones before Zameer, but now they are alert, in fact, they are waiting...waiting for you to go online again.'

Nicole finds it funny, 'That's interesting, you would have to be in it with me... you know.'

A chill passes through Vikram telling him that he fears this woman as intensely as he is attracted to her. Nicole laughs instantly, recognizing his fear. 'The butterflies in your stomach, the increase in your heart rate, the buzzing in your head—is it love or fear Vikram?'

Vikram has no response. She is able to read him like a book. Just a word or look from her is enough to completely destabilize him. This was going to be his new life! He focuses on regulating his breath. *Breathe in...breathe out...not so fast...slow down, innnn, outttt.*

Nicole has pulled out her mobile phone, there is no reception. She steps out of the cave and finds a sweet spot. Logs on, she is checking her bank account. He comes out, can see over her shoulder.

It's a bank account with the balance showing nearly eight million dollars.

51

Raptor Rising

Zzzaaappp.

Vikram tasers Nicole. The pencil-thin taser that looked like a pen was in plain sight, latched to his jacket.

The hi-voltage blast rages through Nicole. Her breath locks, her heart freezes. She doubles up, stumbles behind and starts sinking to the ground. Her eyes are blazing with shock and anger. How could she have missed it! Breathe, she has just moments before he attacks again. But the breath is stuck…it's as though her lungs, her heart are caught in a vice-like grip…

Vikram is trembling, his eyes wide with fear and confusion. It's clear that he acted before thinking and is now unsure of what to do next. Her fingers, holding her mobile phone, open up in a reflex action. It falls to the ground.

He is conscious that she didn't collapse like Rumana: she is still half-standing. And her eyes are still sharply focused. That's not supposed to happen. There is no knowing what she is capable of enduring. He needs to get her down…now… Now, before she recovers…before she…

He tasers her again, *Zzaapp…*

And again, *Zappp… Zaapp…*

This time she is knocked out… collapses, twitching, jerking, the extra shots making her nervous system go crazy. Vikram is white with fear. *Calm down, calm down, get a grip of yourself. It's done…move it… Move now, there is no time to lose.*

He grabs the mobile phone lying on the ground. The screen is still active. A quick look confirms that her account is still open. He looks down at her, ensures she is really knocked out. His breath is jagged, his fingers are trembling. He starts searching for the commands to make the transaction on the website.

Initiate online transfer.

Account number. He punches his account number.

Name. Vikram Singh Shekhat… Shit! He is so freaking nervous he misspells his name, types again.

He wants all the money. He is stealing all the money. The website is taking its own time to respond. Every moment seems like an eternity to him. Damn, damn, damn…

The darkness in Nicole's brain opens for fleeting moments, she takes in the whole scene in a disjointed, hazy, stretched time manner.

Processing….the handset says.

Vikram looks down at Nicole, makes a decision. He can't let her live, he has to act now, before she awakens. He starts rolling her, half-dragging her to the edge.

'I am sorry, I am really sorry, I didn't think… I hadn't really planned to do this…but right now, when you joked about me in the film with you…and your account…the money…it just…happened…' he keeps talking, justifying, unable to stop himself.

She slips out of his hands, he grabs one leg and continues to haul her.

'…but now… it's done…what else can I do? I can't let you live.'

Ping! *Ping*! Initiate fingerprint verification, appears on the screen of her mobile phone.

'Shit.'

A fingerprint verification pad opens up on the touch screen.

On the ground, Nicole is still knocked out, eyes glazed, seemingly unseeing, body still twitching, grunts and groans escaping. Vikram grabs Nicole's twitching hand and jams it open. He can't hold it in place. So he sits on her, holding her down with all his strength.

The unexpectedness of his own response and situation has sizzled his brain. He is struggling to fight through and keep his thoughts clear. His fear of her is rising in waves inside him. Gripped by hysteria, unaware that he is rambling.

'I really meant every word I said. I am completely fascinated by you, I am in love with you, I had really meant to be with you…but once I saw you…as yourself…I am so fucking frightened of you. You are just… like that volcano…were you really joking about killing me? Did you mean it? How the fuck do I know!' his voice is turning into a high pitch scream.

He pins her right arm to the ground with his knee. He is working really hard to meticulously press one twitching finger after another for the fingerprint recognition.

Words pour out of him unchecked, 'How can I spend the rest of my life not knowing when you will yank my neck open? Can any man handle it? Tell me can any…'

Two more fingers to go, he suddenly realizes that she has stopped twitching. He flies off her body as though stung.

'Three shots are enough to knock down a horse, what the hell are you?'

He tasers her again and again. *Zzzaappp, Zzaaappp.*

Nicole's body disjointedly jumps into the air. With great difficulty, he grabs her hand again and completes the prints.

A pre-programmed voice responds, 'Verification in progress… please wait…'

He is afraid even of her unconscious body. One eye on her,

one on the open website processing the payment. The silence is getting to him.

'My Vidya...actually she died five years ago, but I kept her alive... I couldn't let her go. An accident... but why the fuck did she have to do these fucked up things? Never bothered to think about me... What was I supposed to do if something happened to her? I thought once she was dead, I would want to be dead too... but the opposite happened, I was gripped by an intense desire to live...to be alive...every moment. Your energy, the violence made me feel alive, on the edge...it made me love you...'

He is dragging her closer and closer to the cliff's edge.

'When I saw your face I felt I was looking at the most important face in my life... maybe it was that...which gave me the strength to pull the plug on Vidya...and it's the same damn face which I have to destroy to live...cause I am going to live... really live now, on my own terms, far away... free of being a twin, a friend, a stupid cop, of taking dumb arse orders from Raghav...'

The processing sign goes off.

He drags her body the last few feet to the edge of the cliff and starts kicking it, to roll it over. She starts rolling over.

Ping! The account is asking for eyeball recognition.

Vikram curses loudly, dives and grabs her even as she slip-slides half over the edge. A moment later she would have fallen off. The rubble under her is giving way, falling down, bouncing on the rocks deep below.

He jams his foot onto a rock and pulls with all his strength. She is dead weight.

He is gasping for breath, with great difficulty he manages to stop her from rolling off, half drags, half carries her back to the safe ledge again. There are sweat beads running down the stubble on his head, the artery on the temple is visibly throbbing. The count down for the transaction shows only forty-five more seconds.

He is running out of time.

Her body is twitching again, spasms ridding through its entire length. He can barely hold her down, and her eyes are tightly closed. She is lying on her stomach. He sits on her back and yanks back her head. Pries open her eye. Then tries to hold it steady in front of the handset's screen camera. It's practically impossible.

Inside Nicole, a discipline learnt long ago has kicked in. She is chanting something, it's still just a disjointed murmur: something inside her is waking up.

Vikram keeps talking breathlessly, 'I love you. I really do, it's just that I love myself more, the money more...' He jams her head between his legs then holds it in front of the camera again.

The years of training that Shiro put her through, the body's discipline to disregard pain is surfacing. She feels Shiro's presence pervading inside her. This is how a true teacher lives on...

Live.

In her head the chant is reverberating clearer and stronger by the minute, her lips are now attempting to form the words.

On the outside, Vikram hears it as gasps and grunts, more proof of her being knocked out. He is holding her neck at breaking point, eye pried open with his fingers.

Yes, he got it, he thinks he's got it.

Verifying, verifying...rejected, only half the eyeball had been visible.

Vikram cries aloud in anguish. He has gone crazy, with fear, greed and the desperate urgency of the moment. Vile and ugly, his face is that of a demon. He is battering her in frustration, apologizing all the time, declaring love all the time.

Something inside her is getting stronger, in the depths of her mind she realizes that she must not let him know she is recovering.

'Come on, come on, come on…' Vikram mutters desperately.

Last fifteen seconds left. He rolls her over, sits on her stomach. Pries open her eyes with one hand. He is jamming down her body, keeping her convulsions in control. He is completely focused on aligning the handset to her eyes.

Yes. Yes. Her eyes are fully open now. It's steady, it's steady….

Eyeball verification complete. Transfer initiated.

Thud.

He is thrown off at the same time he realizes the significance of the steady eyeball. She has come out of the shock. In a fraction, the tables are turned, he is screeching in fear and pain as she jams her hand on his throat. Then stops.

Vikram sputters, she has lost her nerve. She is still swaying, her awareness is still floating in and out, now is his chance, he reaches inside his jacket for the taser again… she beats him to it, she grabs the taser and flings it away in one motion.

Vikram is doing his best to slither away, away from her. Wham! Blackout.

52

Freedom

Vikram regains consciousness. It's the sudden sharp pain in the chest that wakes him up with a gagging response. She had hit him near his heart, the blow penetrating into its sensory receptors so sharply that he came back to consciousness.

She is ripping off his clothes. It takes him a few moments to gather his wits, once again he is trying to get away: she won't let him. He screams, knowing there is no one in the darkness to hear his screams. She gets him into position, then pinning him down starts kissing him gently, disarming him in spite of himself.

Vikram knows the ritual, tries to buy himself time, starts responding to her. Soon they are rolling over the ground in a frenzy, she allows him to change positions any way he chooses.

The heat of the sex and the fact that she allows him to change positions, always following his leads, lulls Vikram. She isn't wearing her bracelet either, she doesn't have the diamond fangs to puncture his lumber area and paralyse his lower body. The ground is too hard for it to be buried underneath. And she hasn't once caressed his torso to feel out the nerve centres.

As long as he stays on top and keeps a tight grip on her hips, he is safe. He is on top of her once again. This is where she is supposed to start, she hasn't. He feels strangely elated. Laughs.

Wham! The laughter chokes inside him.

In one smooth motion, she lifts her entire body along with him... thud.... When they land back he is on the ground and she is on top. The breath is knocked out of him.

Time extends. In less than the time it takes for him to inhale again, her hands are moving on his torso, the sickeningly familiar movement of the death ritual. She did not need to caress to find his nerve points, she has already studied his body when he was knocked out. She is making sharp jabs and hits, stunning and paralysing different parts of his body.

His brain moves faster than his body, his brain recognizes death.

She breaks the ritual to bend down and whisper to him, 'I hadn't planned to kill you...you were not worthy...' she laughs. 'Then you elevated your status!'

Hit on the heart. Vikram's eyes mist over with unshed tears the same as Zameer's. But he is not listening to Nicole any more.

He can hear Vidya call...call him out to play...he has to go...

Vikram is already running out... Vidya is calling again... impatient...

When Nicole's fingers plunge to his neck... he smiles. Their eyes lock, it seems like an eternity, she is the demon, the goddess... his entire universe...it's only a fraction of a moment.

Contact. Darkness... Freedom...

Nicole yanks out the jugular, spurting blood, she throws back her head and screams. A full-throated animal cry of victory, recognized by all species across all time.

Her silhouette, an exact match to the image of the Garou.

She drags Vikram's body to the spot from where he tried to push her over. One push and he goes over the edge, his backpack follows him into a gorge. She looks over the ledge, the seeping lava will burn the body and the small backpack, destroying all traces forever.

She opens her handset, starts editing. She had filmed Vikram's killing just like the others. She rapidly edits herself out. Nicole does a last check on the film. All ok.

Upload.

On another website, the five million starts pouring in, this time as Bitcoins. Within moments, the transactions are complete. The sites start garbling.

Nicole freezes.

Something stirred in the shadows behind her... to know, to recognize before you see... she smiles. It's Shiro, he is back.

She will never again need CMND-Z blocked.

She steps into the shadows. She is home.

The occasional flare of the volcano lights up the sky.

Epilogue

London.

Smith mulls over a video, it's the screen recording of Vikram's kill film. Uploaded twenty minutes ago. His mobile pings. The quantum key for CMND-Z blocked has been received.

Nicole has kept her promise.

He had been surprised when he got her call from Vikram's mobile phone. The video should be buried. That was her price for the key.

He had been even more surprised by her amazing naivety when she said, 'Use it to do good.'

He almost laughed out loud. This was a strange woman indeed, a cold-blooded killer yet 'good' still existed in her world. It sure as hell didn't exist in his.

He marks the video for archival. Nobody is going to see it. He will keep his side of the bargain.

◆

Mumbai.

Raghav's office.

He firmly closes the door behind him. The press conference had not gone well. His jowls are still wobbling with the suppressed rage the questions had elicited. That damn Vikram, it had been a mistake to rope him in.

And now the bastard was untraceable. Could be dead. Maybe Smith had missed it… Maybe. Fuck Vikram. He wanted out. His request for transfer was already on the minister's desk…

He found himself staring at his favourite screensaver once again. The killer astride Zameer. 'Come on… just one more time…'

Tashi was made of sterner stuff. She had started at the beginning all over again. One thing she knew, she couldn't touch Nicole. Nicole's face on Zameer's killer had to remain discredited. Else, someday, her own face on Khurana's killer would come to haunt her. Her own face wearing the club crimson lipstick.

Poor Khurana had been declared missing and would remain missing.

◆

Kīlauea.

A large slow sure-footed figure starts an upward journey towards the far-off volcano. Michael. He stops to take a breather. Turns around to look at the path he is leaving behind.

Little does Michael Paddington, the great-grandson of Atiq Khan, know that he is living that long-ago day when Atiq looked over Irshad Pass for the last time. Like Atiq, he is making his way to a future he least expects.

The true student will come seeking the master.

Acknowledgements

Mani Shankar, for the many amazingly diverse screenplay collaborations we have worked on, over the years. *Raptor Rising* being inspired by one such screenplay.

Indebted to the team at Rupa Publications for publishing *Raptor Rising*.

Kingshuk Nag, for his encouragement and guidance.